CHRISTMAS AT NELSON RANCH

The Texas Two-Step Series

KATHY CARMICHAEL

MacGowan Press

CHRISTMAS AT NELSON RANCH

Kathy Lynch Carmichael

Copyright © 2021 by Kathy Lynch Carmichael

FREE DOWNLOAD

**READ THE LOVE STORY
THAT STARTED IT ALL ...**

Sign up for the author's Readers Group News email list and receive a **free** digital copy of *Western Pleasure (The Texas Two-Step Series) Novella.*

Visit KathyCarmichael.com to sign up

Email: Kathy@KathyCarmichael.com

Web: http://www.KathyCarmichael.com

Twitter: http://www.twitter.com/kathycarmichael

Facebook: http://www.facebook.com/kathycarmichael

FOREWORD

Basically, I created a fiend. An attention fiend. When my husband wrote a Foreword for my *Heaven and the Afterlife* book, he liked it. He liked it too much.

He did a great job and received all kinds of praise (deservedly so). This, I'm afraid, went to his head. Especially when the book sold well, he began telling people (bragging) that he was now a bestselling author.

So.

Fast forward to now. I do mean Foreword.

He's written one—or at least started to write one. I give you, John Carmichael:

It was a dark and scary night. The wind was howling and it was starting to rain. She had to get home fast—before her nightmare came true—or was she too late?

Okay. That was it. I hope you enjoyed it as much as I did (like the wind, I was howling). Please tell others how much you enjoyed his Forward. He'll love it!

Thank you!

Kathy Carmichael (someone please help me)

PRAISE FOR THE FOREWORD

Praise for the **Foreword** to *Christmas at Nelson Ranch!*

"Attention Getting!" ~ Vicki Hinze, USA Today bestselling author of *Down and Dead in Dixie*

"Perfectly spelled!" ~ Maggie Shayne, *New York Times* bestselling author of *FATAL, BUT FESTIVE*

"Refreshingly brief!" ~ Brenda Hiatt, *New York Times* bestselling author of the *Starstruck series*

"Very descriptive!" ~ Terri West, Reader and Proud Grandmother

"Praise worthy!" ~ Robin Kenny, Overlord of all Words Ending in "Q"

"Did I detect a Scottish accent?" ~ Karla Stoker, Retired Corporate Senior Leader, Full time Wife/Mother/Grandmother

"Sgoinneil!"* ~ Denise Lynn, bestselling author of *DREAM KNIGHT*

    **Sgoinneil in Scots Gaelic means brilliant, smashing.*

"I have notes..." ~ Kimberly Llewellyn, bestselling author

PROLOGUE

San Antonio, Texas
   Twenty-five years ago

Harlan Nelson had come this far and he wasn't about to die now.

The night was impenetrably dark, with clouds blacking out the stars. An eerie three-quarter moon was veiled in ebony wisps and even the wind had stopped howling. The scent of mildew permeated the hot muggy air, calling up images of long-dead monks. Hot, still, quiet.

Too quiet.

The only sound came from Harlan's own heavy breathing and his captor's footsteps on the hardened earth behind him.

Harlan stumbled over broken bricks that at one

time made up the walls at the Espada Mission in southern San Antonio. A sharp brick gouged deep into his hip. Pain shot down his leg. His ankle twisted, but he was far more worried about the gun aimed dead center on his forehead.

"Get up."

His heart pounding, Harlan heaved himself to a crouch. He had to find a way out. Had to escape. All he needed was one chance to break into a run. He was fast. Surely that would be an advantage? Just one chance.

If he rushed the lowlife, would he survive? He had to wait for the right time, when it wouldn't be expected.

Standing upright, he tried to get his bearings. The night was dark enough. If he made a run for the chapel, he stood a good chance of evading his captor. He made out an archway to the right, but they were walking in the other direction. Were they heading toward the lime kilns?

"Turn back to the left." The gun glinted in the feeble moonlight as it pointed the way.

Definitely the kilns. Not good.

Harlan did as he was told, promising himself that he *would* make it back home. He *would* return to Whispering Lake to attend his wife and newborn baby's graveside service. He *would* find a way.

"Stop there."

The attacker intended to kill him. Harlan hadn't been led to this remote corner of the mission for amusement or mere effect.

Breathe. Remain calm. There had to be a way to delay the inevitable. One chance.

Confrontation was risky, but the odds had been completely stacked against him from the beginning. It was his only hope. Spinning to face the assailant, Harlan asked, "You think that mask fools me? I know exactly who you are."

His attacker was a black shadow in the ruins. "It doesn't change a thing."

Did Harlan notice some hesitation? Maybe it wasn't the end. "Look. I won't say anything. Just let me go and we'll forget this ever happened."

"You're right. This never happened." The assailant laughed, sending waves of fear through Harlan's veins.

"Are you crazy?" he demanded. What did his attacker have to gain? For the last two days, since Harlan had learned of the death of his wife and newborn baby, he'd made his way back from the oilrig he worked on in the gulf toward home, desperate to be there for the funeral. It would take a lot more than a bullet to stop him. He needed to make amends, even if it was too little, too late. "You're not going to get away with this."

The shadow didn't move.

"If you're going to shoot me, I deserve to know why."

"Don't you think you've done enough damage?" The attacker aimed the gun directly at Harlan's head. "Say your prayers."

There was a lot to be said for prayer. *Please God, if I fail let me join Wendy and Holly in heaven. Let them forgive me.*

Then Harlan made his move, lunging for the assailant's gun arm.

A shot rang out.

He hadn't been fast enough.

He'd never go home again.

CHAPTER ONE

Fort Worth, Texas
Current Day

Holly Brown had spent most of her nearly twenty-five years wondering who she was. Now she wished she didn't know.

According to Slade Colfax, seated beside her in her adoptive dad's home office, her birth parents were Harlan and Wendy Nelson. He'd come to Fort Worth because Holly's biological grandmother, Tammie Dean, wanted to meet her.

Holly shot Slade a glare, fully aware she wouldn't resent him so much if her dad wasn't sending her away. In fact, up until three days ago, she would have been thrilled.

If only there hadn't been a bomb.

Her gaze settled on the boxes of Christmas decorations piled in the corner. She and her dad hadn't yet had time to put up the tree or even to hang a wreath.

Her fingers worried the dark red leather of her wing chair. She'd always loved the tender chats she and her dad had shared in this very room. It was a place of warmth and comfort.

And the Christmas season was even more special.

Now the room felt cold and surreal. The bottom had dropped out of her world and she couldn't quite make sense of anything.

"I will admit, Slade, your timing couldn't be better," continued her dad, Alfred Brown. "Finding any information about Holly's birth has been next to impossible."

Talk about an understatement. Her dad had retired as Fort Worth District Attorney five years earlier and through the years all the resources at his disposal hadn't turned up any facts about her birth parents.

The only information her dad knew came from the adoption agency when he received the call telling him they were bringing him a baby girl. The baby's family had chosen him and her mom expressly from the vast pool of potential parents. They specifically wanted the Browns to become Holly's parents.

While it had been a comfort to know her birth family cared enough to choose who would raise her, she'd always wondered exactly why, if they'd cared so much, they had given her up. It would always hurt, knowing she hadn't been wanted. It was especially painful after the death of her mom when she'd been twelve years old.

She and her father had gotten by okay on their own, but there had been times she would have loved to have had a grandmother to turn to.

She narrowed her eyes at Slade Colfax. Her dad was wrong. Slade couldn't have come into her life at a worse time.

He shifted, and his gaze challenged hers, as if he knew she'd been glaring at him. His eyes were a deep gray with a smattering of green flecks near the irises. In any other situation she would have found him wildly attractive rather than maddeningly intrusive.

If she was bluntly honest with herself, she *was* attracted to him and annoyed with herself for being so.

Her father must have sensed it, because he back-tracked and said, "Tell me again how you're related to Holly."

Slade's gaze left hers and she felt—relieved and maybe, a little—lonely.

"We're not related, sir," Slade replied. "I was raised by my aunt who married into the Nelson family when I was three. Even though there's no blood relation, I look on Tammie Dean as if I were one of her grandkids, and she returns the affection."

He turned back to Holly. "She's apparently kept an eye on you all these years."

Holly saw red. If her grandmother had kept an eye on her, the woman would have known that after the death of her mom, Holly needed a woman in her life. Apparently she wasn't important enough to console in her time of grief. "Why now? Why is she contacting me now?"

The cowboy's jaw tightened, almost imperceptibly—but she noticed.

Good. She was glad he was nervous.

"She didn't say this," he answered, "but I suspect it's because she had a taste of her own mortality. Tammie Dean lived life as if would never end until recently. She had a stroke. We all thought we were going to lose her."

"And she asked for me afterward?"

He nodded. "Said she wasn't ready to meet her maker, but she *was* ready to meet her granddaughter."

Her timing, not Holly's. Resentment welled up inside her until she thought she might burst. "She's in stable condition?"

"As far as we know. The doctor's running more tests to make sure, but it looks as if medication and an improved diet will do the trick."

"So there's no emergency." Holly faced her dad. She didn't have to go immediately. She could stay and look after her dad. "Meeting my grandmother can wait. I'm not leaving you. Besides, it's Christmas time. I've never spent it away from you."

"You're going. Please, Holly. There can't be any disagreement about this." Her dad looked down at his hands for a moment. When he raised his head again, his expression was serious and intent.

Her heart sank.

He addressed the cowboy. "And you and your wife will take care of Holly? Keep her safe?"

"Sorry, sir," said Slade. "I'm single. But I promise to look after your girl."

Her dad turned back to face her again. "Until the bomber is caught, you will stay away."

With the worry lines etching his face, for once he showed every day of his seventy-five years. "I want you safe. We don't know who is targeting me, but apparently he's willing to kill any number of people to get at me. You're not going to be collateral damage."

Holly shook her head, determined to change his mind. Her dad being targeted was all the more reason to remain by his side. She didn't have to go, no matter what he said. He couldn't force her to leave town. Unfortunately, he was stubborn enough to make it impossible for her to look after him.

After his heart attack last year, he needed her. Someone had to make sure he ate properly, exercised, and took his medication. That someone was her, bomber or no bomber. "I'm more concerned about you."

"Do I need to remind you of what happened when you were fifteen?"

His words were like a punch to her stomach and she blanched. No. He didn't need to remind her. She'd never forget the feel of sharp steel against her flesh. But this was a subject they never discussed. Ever.

He, because of guilt, and she, because she never wanted to remember how she'd almost been abducted by one of the felons he'd prosecuted. To bring it up now, in front of a virtual stranger, rankled.

Slade shifted in his seat. Even he was uncomfortable. No matter how much she'd like to, she couldn't very well send him out of the room, and the situation was too serious to dismiss it.

She had to keep her cool. This wasn't about her. It was about her dad.

He had apparently forgotten she was no longer a child, not to mention his precarious physical condition. "Your heart—"

"Last checkup, the doctor said I was doing well."

"But—"

He waved his hand in an effort to silence her. "There's nothing for you to worry about. Law enforcement is all over this. They're putting together a list of recently released perps I sent up. Holly, go to Whispering Lake. I need you safe."

"I'm going to look after your daughter, sir." Slade planted his boot-clad feet firmly on the floor, looking every inch the cowboy he claimed to be, then stood. "She'll be in good hands."

"I know she will." Her father crossed from behind his desk and approached Holly, placing a hand on her knee. "The FBI checked into the Nelson's and they're honest and honorable. Despite having given you up, they're good people. Slade will make sure you don't come to any harm."

"It's not going to happen, Dad." Holly bristled. The last thing she wanted was for the "men folk" to look after her. If she could corral a classroom of ten year olds, she could look after herself. "I have to be back at school—"

"Not until mid-January. By then you'll have had a wonderful opportunity to meet your birth family and the bomber will be behind bars. You'll be back in plenty of time for classes."

"You need me to watch after you. I can't leave you here alone—"

"I won't be alone. Fredericks has promised to stay in the guestroom and the house is under surveillance." He reached out and touched the back of her hand with his fingertips. "I'll watch my diet, Holly. I'll take my medication. You don't have to worry."

"You can say that a thousand times, but it won't make me stop worrying." She bit her lip. "I know you're afraid if I stay behind something will happen to me, but who is going to watch *your* back?"

"Have you counted the number of law enforcement officers in our living room?"

She had to give him that. There were at least two, not to mention the ones staking out the house's exterior. "They're more concerned with catching the bomber than they are with your health. The stress isn't good for you."

"Worrying about you increases my stress ten-fold. If something happened to you because of me, I would never forgive myself. Not after the last time when I nearly lost you."

"But, Dad, I—"

"No." He lifted a hand for her to stop. "If I'm busy watching out for you, I can't watch out for me."

She stilled. How could she argue against that? She couldn't. She...couldn't.

He leaned down and gave her a gentle hug, then released her. "Promise me, Holly, you'll go to Whispering Lake with Slade. Meet your grandmother. Have a wonderful time getting ready for Christmas. I'll rest easy knowing you're in safe hands. With any luck, you'll be back in plenty of time to celebrate."

No argument she came up with would change her father's mind. But she didn't have to go easy on the man who'd put her in such an impossible bind. If Slade hadn't shown up, her dad might not have gotten the bright idea of sending her away.

"I don't want to force you into anything you don't want, Holly," said Slade. "I'm merely giving you the opportunity to meet some of your biological family, especially Tammie Dean who specifically longs to see you."

She considered this for a moment, but wasn't satisfied. "What about my parents, Slade? Why was I given up?"

"You'll find out more when you meet Tammie Dean.

I can promise you she wouldn't have allowed it if she didn't have a very good reason." He tapped his Stetson against his jeans clad leg. "Tammie Dean doesn't make decisions lightly, not when it comes to family."

It wasn't much of an answer, but it was probably all she would get until she could ask her grandmother in person. "I'm calling you every night, Dad."

"I wouldn't have it any other way."

She sighed, not happy, but resigned. "I'll go pack."

Holly's apartment wasn't far from her father's house, and Slade had been relieved when it hadn't taken her long to get her things together. They were making good time and had already been on the road for an hour.

It was warm for early December. It was the time of year where you couldn't count on the weather being cold or hot. One minute it would be sweltering and the next freezing.

That day wasn't record breaking, but sultrier than usual for the time of year. Slade was glad he'd taken his grandmother's sedan rather than his truck. It was more comfortable for passengers and the heat and air conditioner worked well. City girls like their comfort.

No good was going to come of bringing Holly to the Nelson Ranch. Like water and oil, spoiled city girls and rough West Texas ranching don't mix. He knew that from firsthand experience.

Holly pulled her sweater around her shoulders. Was she chilled or merely worried? Since they'd left she'd barely said three words.

"Want me to adjust the temperature?"

"That's okay. I'm just anxious."

He could have told her that with the way she chewed her lip and fidgeted in her seat.

Meeting her had been enlightening. He'd have recognized her as a Nelson, even if he hadn't already known. She resembled her grandmother in many ways, including the same mulish expression when she didn't want to do something.

"I just hope Dad will be okay."

"I'm sure he will. He won't be as stressed with you in Whispering Lake."

She might not admit it, but she was better off with Slade at the Nelson ranch, far from the threat of harm. He just hoped she wouldn't be bored. With her trendy skirt and high heels, she looked every inch what she was.

Cute but citified.

He'd already been there and done that with a pampered big city girl. His ex-fiancée had been from Dallas where they'd met when he'd visited while on business. A whirlwind romance and one engagement ring later, he'd brought her home to meet the family and to see the place she'd soon call home.

The romance quickly fizzled. He'd known it from the first moment she'd entered the barn and turned up her nose at the smell. The minor cracks in their relationship grew into huge crevices. But he was a man of his word, so he'd stuck with it.

Her fleeing back to Dallas had been a relief, except rather than breaking his heart, it broke Tammie Dean's. She had welcomed his fiancée wholeheartedly and finding the note his fiancée had left that said little more than thanks for the lousy memories, devastated her. She got hopping mad when the woman said she knew he wouldn't want his ring back and hadn't returned it.

Showed how little his ex-fiancée knew about him. The ring had been his mother's, which she'd worn until her death. It had taken seven months and almost the same number in thousands of dollars to get the heirloom back.

But he'd gotten it back.

He wouldn't easily give it away again and definitely not to some metropolitan girl. He'd had his fill of them and then some.

If they don't have a surplus of shops and excitement, they grow bored.

Whispering Lake was a small West-Texas town. The closest large town was Abilene and even it couldn't truly be described as a big city like Fort Worth. But it was big enough for their requirements, and when it wasn't, there was always Dallas and Fort Worth.

Although there was plenty of family for her to meet, Holly would likely end up spending many hours at the bedside of an older woman she didn't know.

She'd quickly grow weary from the lack of things to do. Then he'd be stuck trying to buy her off with a trip to Europe or something even more extravagant. One look at the ranch, and Holly would see dollar signs, just as his ex had. City girls were all gloss and no substance.

What had Tammie Dean been thinking?

Or had she been thinking at all?

When she'd finally woken up from the stroke, she'd seemed like her usual cheerful self. Everyone had been thankful that her memory had been unscathed, and the only damage seemed to be a weakness of her right side. She just needed time to recuperate.

Everyone thought she was in good mental shape until she asked for her granddaughter. Slade's cousin, Marie, was already in the large, private hospital room. They'd been raised together, and he thought of her as one might think of a pesky little sister.

She'd stepped forward. "I'm here, Gran."

"Not you, dear. I want Holly."

Uncle Daryl, the youngest of Tammie Dean's four children, stood up from his chair in the corner of the room. He was in his mid-fifties, but looked much younger. "What are you talking about, Mom?"

"Where's Slade?" she asked.

He'd approached the foot of her bed. "I'm here."

"I want you to go get Holly."

He hadn't known how to answer. It wasn't until later that day, when they were alone, that she'd explained about Holly.

Slade had been stunned by the news, yet there was nothing Tammie Dean could ask of him that he could ever refuse, including being the one to inform the rest of the family that Holly was still alive. They hadn't taken it very well, and he assumed that was why Tammie Dean hadn't wanted to tell them herself.

Because he was so busy with necessary ranching tasks, he couldn't immediately grant Tammie Dean's request to meet her granddaughter. As soon as possible, he'd headed to Fort Worth to meet Holly and her dad.

Slade had been worried about what he would find, half expecting Holly's Dad to send him packing. Instead, Slade had given the man his word that he would move heaven and earth to protect that man's only child. Holly.

Although she had an innocent look about her, Slade doubted it. Perhaps as a schoolteacher she hadn't spent much time in the real world, but again he doubted it. She was far too pretty with long, golden hair and dazzling blue eyes that probably twinkled when she wasn't so worried.

The minute he'd clapped eyes on her he'd had mixed feelings about bringing her to meet Tammie Dean. A small voice inside him warned that it was a mistake taking her to the ranch, and one he'd come to regret. He tried ignoring it. Yet the inner voice persisted, reminding him that city girls were nothing but trouble.

But Tammie Dean wanted her and what she wanted

he would provide. He just hoped Holly wasn't bringing a world of trouble with her to Whispering Lake.

He asked, "Would some music on the radio help take your mind off things?"

She really looked at him for the first time since they'd left her father's office, her eyes a troubled blue that reminded him of the wide, Texas sky on a stormy, summer day. She shook her head. "But maybe instead you could tell me a little about my grandmother and my biological parents?"

His day was now perfect—perfectly rotten. It was going to be up to him to explain that, like him, she too was an orphan.

CHAPTER TWO

Whispering Lake, Texas

The one thing Bridget Nelson Wilson couldn't tolerate was scandal. Just like a Texas tornado, a scandal was brewing right now, and she could do little to stop it.

She was on a damage-control mission and as a result, she parked her car in front of her niece, Marie Nelson's, quilting shop.

Bridget's son, Max, as town sheriff, had gone to San Antonio to identify the remains of her older brother, Harlan. He'd come back with confirmation that Harlan had died twenty-five years earlier.

At the news, all she'd felt was relief that the family black sheep would never return to make more trouble. Harlan had never been anything except bad news.

Scandal upon scandal, the man was a disgrace, even in death.

Bridget exited the car and stepped up the curb onto the sidewalk in front of the shops lining Main Street. The shops had all been decorated with tinsel, greenery, and whatever other Christmas monstrosity they considered tasteful. Although the winter solstice hadn't yet arrived, the temperature had already begun cooling. Despite that, she wiped moisture forming on her brow.

It was far too steamy for just before Christmas, exactly like the truths and half-truths about her family. She'd thought she could weather this storm by ignoring it, but what she hadn't taken into account was her mother's reaction to the news that Harlan's body had been found.

First the stroke, and then the demand that Slade fetch Harlan's lovechild. They'd all believed the girl was dead.

Lord-a-mercy, it was Scandal with a capital S.

If only she'd anticipated Mama's reaction. She'd certainly have ensured the news of Harlan's death was kept from her.

But she hadn't. Now Tammie Dean was making noises about a memorial service. After Harlan had run off all those years ago and not a word to his family?

Give me a break, she seethed.

Didn't matter that he'd died back then. If the news didn't set the town tongues to wagging, she didn't know anything. Not to mention the return of his lovechild.

Technically the girl's parents were married, but she was the next thing to being born outside of wedlock. She'd barely squeaked in.

And here she was, come back to life.

Now Bridget would have to suffer all the humiliation once more. The girl would be fine. Bridget was the one who would be forced to tolerate the fallout—pitying glances, snickers and whispers behind her back—again.

Not to mention her husband, Jameson's reaction. While he was a fine family man, he didn't much like the idea of adding additional members to it.

She let out a long-suffering sigh. The foolishness she had to put up with from her family was a disgrace. Unfair, awful, disgrace.

Tammie Dean had made sure Harlan married the girl's mother before he ran off. Wendy. She was one of those no-account Farradays and was scared of her own shadow. Those Farradays didn't have two nickels to rub together. They were lower than low on the social totem pole.

What had Harlan been thinking, messing around with a girl like that?

When Wendy's father found out she was pregnant, he'd beaten her within an inch of her life. Harlan had toted her, beaten and bloody, to their mother for help. It was no wonder Tammie Dean decided to rescue the girl and welcomed her into the family home. Her mama never could bear watching others suffer.

Bridget didn't have time for girls like Wendy. Never

did. Back then she'd been far too busy to pay much attention, what with planning her wedding to Jameson.

Jameson Wilson had been a great catch. He'd been dangling around, too shy to propose like the usual cowboys, and she'd liked that about him. So when she suggested he marry her, she'd only had one stipulation—there would be no scandal ever attached to his name.

He'd been barely out of college and had just gotten his Certified Public Accountant license. Marrying into the Nelson family would set him up for life ,and he was smart enough to know it. It hadn't taken him ten seconds to get down on his knees, promise her the world, and beg her to marry him.

Bridget smiled. The memory was sweet.

Even better had been Georgette Larson's expression when Bridget told her. Bridget knew Georgette had her heart set on Jameson. He was *that* handsome, so who could blame her? There was nothing better than one-upping a member of the Larson family.

The feud between the Nelsons and the Larsons extended back before the town was founded in 1875. The Larsons were known as hotheaded, but even lumped as a bunch, they weren't as steely determined as Bridget. Besting Georgette had been a driving force in Bridget's life.

If she wanted to limit the damage done to the family name, facing the gossips at the quilting shop was her best chance of success. Especially before Georgette got wind of it.

Why, oh, why, did Bridget have to go through this mortification? It's not as if she'd personally done anything to justify it. Her life would be far more agreeable if only Harlan's daughter would return to the grave she'd crawled out of.

With that encouraging thought, she yanked open the over-the-top-decorated-and-embellished glass doors facing Main Street and entered the den of gossip iniquity.

In just a few short hours, Holly had gone from being a twosome with her dad to having a huge family of aunts, uncles, cousins, and a grandmother. How disappointing that neither of her biological parents was alive. Slade could have been a little kinder in the way he'd told her.

"They've both kicked the bucket," he had said, then he'd changed the subject.

Maybe it was a typical male reaction, trying to avoid anything the least bit unpleasant. She suspected it was more likely that he regretted having to be the bearer of bad news.

Either way, she couldn't let his attitude get to her. A large extended family still alive and kicking waited for her to meet. After a lifetime of wondering, the time had finally arrived to find out where she really came from and possibly bring closure to the questions she had her whole life.

When Slade turned off the freeway onto a rural highway, she thrummed with excitement. The only thing keeping her from complete joy was concern about her dad.

"Look up ahead." Slade pointed toward a massive, brick-gated entrance. "It's the main gate to the Nelson Ranch."

The brick entrance was grand—an edifice—over twenty feet tall and about fifty feet in length. At the highest part of the arch above the road, wrought iron work spelled out the words "Nelson Ranch." Boughs of fresh evergreens had been twined around the entrance stonework, already decorated for the season.

"Nice greenery," she said.

Slade colored. "We don't know when Tammie Dean will be coming home, so I wanted something to welcome her."

"You did a good job." She pointed toward the little unlit twinkle lights. "I hope she gets to see the lights when she comes home, too."

He nodded, apparently embarrassed by his efforts to please Tammie Dean.

"When you said my family was primarily made up of ranchers, I'd imagined a quaint little farm house with some cows—not this." She spread her hands to indicate the gates and everything around the broad and mostly flat countryside.

He met her gaze and held it, as though trying to

discern her thoughts. "It is impressive. I remember the first time I saw it when I was a kid."

He halted in front of the archway, allowing Holly the chance to take it all in. "I was jumping up and down excited. I couldn't believe it when my aunt and new uncle brought me to the land of cowboys and Indians."

Holly swallowed, a sliver of intimidation inching its way down her throat. "How big is this place?"

"Twenty thousand acres, give or take."

Huge. Good heavens. She took in the twisting road leading up a small hill covered with mesquite trees, even some cactus. It was gorgeous. "Is that an oil well over there?"

He nodded. "It's called a pumpjack. When I first saw one, I thought it was a giant black ant. I told my mother, and she said it was pumping black gold. You'll see a number of them on the ranch."

All the blood drained out of her face. Now she was completely intimidated. All this land *and* oil.

He watched her carefully, and somehow she got the impression that her response had disappointed him in some way.

Just then a sedan came toward them from the ranch, churning up dust and gravel as it neared. It didn't slow when it reached them, instead the driver sped up and turned onto the rural highway.

"That was your uncle—Jameson Wilson. He's married to your Aunt Bridget."

"Friendly guy." She hadn't been able to make out

much through the tinted car windshield, other than dark hair and a scowl.

"Probably just busy with all the hoopla related to Tammie Dean being in the hospital. He's a CPA and handles all of the Nelson Ranch finances.

"Is Tammie Dean at the ranch? Was he visiting her? Will I meet her now?"

He shook his head. "Although she's doing fine, they're keeping her in the hospital for tests. But you might meet your cousin, Lucas Wilson. When your grandfather, Conrad Nelson, passed away, Lucas came home and has been running the ranch ever since. Tammie Dean had a modern ranch house built adjacent to the main ranch house for Lucas."

"So he's not in the main house?"

"He lives in his ranch house. No one's living in the main house right now, until Tammie Dean comes home. She told me to put you in the old homestead. It's been fixed up as a guest cottage."

Guest cottage? Main house? Ranch house? Her stomach cramped with tension.

"Don't be nervous." He must have seen something in her expression to give away her misgivings. "They won't bite."

"I just hope they like me—and the reverse. I want to love them."

"What's not to love?"

She shot him a look, but he wasn't sure how to read it.

"Ready?" he asked.

Holly cleared her throat, taking one last look at the entrance. "Ready as I'll ever be."

Slade turned the sedan onto the sandy dirt road and slowly drove up the rise. As he reached the top, she saw a sweeping panorama of fields, outbuildings, winding dirt roads and, in the distance, a sprawling house built of native stone with several other buildings nearby. "Is that the main house?"

"Yes. Lucas's place is on the left and the old homestead is not too far off, over that way to the right." He swung his arm to indicate the direction and house he meant.

It was a good distance from the other buildings. She viewed the two-story reddish-orange brick house with a silvery aluminum roof that matched the roof of the other houses, then she looked back toward the left. "Which one of the cottages is yours?"

"I've got my own spread not too far from here." He shrugged.

"If it's half as nice as this, I'm sure it's lovely."

"More like one twentieth—it's just a few hundred acres." Again he eyed her warily, then abruptly cleared his throat as if to end the topic. "Once we get you settled in, I thought we could go to the hospital in Abilene to visit Tammie Dean. She's chomping at the bit, wanting to meet you. Afterwards, I'll take you for some dinner. Do you like Mexican food?"

"I love it," she replied as Slade parked in front of the

homestead cottage. "And it's really smart of you to bribe me with it, too."

"Good to know for future reference. *Can be bribed with enchiladas. Check.*" He made a check symbol in the air.

"I may not be as much of a pushover as you hope."

Was the man crazy enough to roll his eyes at her? Surely she was mistaken and it was a only a trick of the light.

"I'm not that easy," she asserted.

"Tell me something I don't already know," he said.

She fought back a response. Okay. Maybe he was right. Maybe she had resisted leaving her dad, but she didn't think she'd been *that* difficult.

She exited the car and climbed the steps to enter the ranch. Inside was surprisingly an open concept. As she stepped into the living room, she saw all the way back to the kitchen and dining rooms. To the right was a staircase and behind it a hall, likely leading to the master bedroom.

Slade brought her bags to the bedroom, then returned to the living area to wait for her.

It didn't take long for her to get situated, then freshen up. As she came back into the cozy living area to join Slade, she spied a photograph of a large wedding group hanging on the staircase wall. At the center the bride and groom stood proudly, surrounded by men, women and children. Even an infant.

Slade walked over to join her. "I didn't know this

was here." He pointed to a man and woman in the group. "That's my aunt and uncle."

The woman held a baby in her arms and standing in front of them was an adorable boy of about five. "Is that you?"

He nodded.

She studied the boy and could see how he could grow into the man who stood beside her. Tall, lean and all muscle. The impish gleam in the boy's eyes seemed to be missing in the man. Sad. What had happened? Had his spirit been broken?

"This here's Tammie Dean." He indicated a woman standing beside the bride. "It's surprising how much you resemble your grandmother. You have the same look about you."

They did share a likeness. While Holly's eyes were blue, Tammie Dean's eyes seemed darker. Brown or hazel? The bride next to her looked little like her, except for the blond hair color. "Who's the bride?"

"Your Aunt Bridget." As if he could read her thoughts he added, "Tammie Dean always said Bridget is the spitting image of her father."

He touched the glass. "That's him. Conrad Nelson."

So that's where Holly had gotten her blue eyes. Although a tall proud man, he leaned heavily on a cane.

"When this was taken, he'd been diagnosed with cancer and had started chemo. It left him weak. Tammie Dean had her hands full, running the ranch, raising her kids and looking after an ailing husband."

Seeing her family for the first time brought a tear to Holly's eyes, but she hurriedly wiped it away. There was something familiar about all of the people in the group. If she'd come across this photo before knowing they were her relatives, would she have felt this same affinity?

"That's Bridget's husband, Jameson Wilson." Slade indicated the groom. "They have three grown boys now. And look over here. That's your mother, just a month or so before her death."

Holly held her breath as she studied the photograph of her mother. Her mother stood at the far edge of the photograph, as if unsure she should be in the picture at all. It was apparent that she was pregnant, but she seemed faded in comparison to all of the Nelsons. A sweet face, blond hair, yet not the kind of woman who would draw your eye like the other blonde in the center of the photo: the bride.

Holly released her breath. What kind of woman was her mother? Was she as sweet as her face? She seemed almost intimidated by having been included in the photograph.

Had her mother lived, would she have sung lullabies to her? She could ask Slade, but she feared the answer. Seeing her family brought to mind the fact the Nelsons had rejected her. Why?

Her gaze snagged on the image of a handsome cowboy, attired in a dark suit, standing next to her mother. Perhaps it was the way he stood with his feet planted wide, but she knew immediately he was a cowboy. He had a bad boy look to him, cocky, as if he might jump on a bucking bronco at any moment and she had no doubt who would win. "Is that my—"

"Your father. Yes."

She eagerly drank in the cowboy's image in the photograph. He had the same blue eyes as her grandfather. As her.

What she would have given for a single conversation with either of her birth parents. Would her father have been strict? Or would he have been a doting papa? Or some combination of the two? From the mischievous grin on his face, she suspected he would have been lots of fun to know. And he would have been amused if she'd ever gotten into trouble.

It's not as though she didn't appreciate and adore her dad who raised her. She did. More than words could express. But she'd always wondered.

"This is probably the last photo ever taken of him," added Slade. "If I recollect rightly, he ran off the very next day."

Ran off? Her throat tightened. Her father hadn't wanted her either.

CHAPTER THREE

Holly ran nervous hands down her pants legs, hoping there wasn't enough perspiration to stain them. As excited as she was about meeting Tammie Dean, she also dreaded the situation. What if her grandmother didn't like her? Or found her wanting in some way?

As they approached her grandmother's hospital room, they heard both a male and female voice. They stepped inside, and she noted a man with dark hair, holding papers under one arm and a stack of file folders beneath the other.

She was pretty sure this was her Uncle Jameson. He looked like a numbers guy—a bit nerdy and buttoned down. He was shorter than Slade—by several inches. And she couldn't help but think Uncle Jameson was aware of his vertical shortcomings.

Perhaps it was in the way he grinned a little too

widely at them. Or maybe it was how his gaze flitted from Slade's to hers and back again.

She wasn't sure, but he hurried out of the room, pausing only to nod at her upon Slade's abbreviated introduction attempt.

Ever since his parents' death, Slade couldn't enter a hospital without morbid thoughts. The antiseptic smells, the muffled voices, and cries of patients, even the feel of the cold, tile floor against his boots brought him back to one of the worst moments of his life.

Hospitals were no place for the living.

As difficult as it was for him to visit Tammie Dean in the hospital, he wouldn't have traded the experience of seeing her reunited with Holly for the world.

After the introduction to Jameson, and Holly and Slade had first entered Tammie Dean's room, Holly hung back for a moment. Tammie Dean's eyes lit up as soon as she caught sight of Holly and she spread her arms wide open. Holly ran to her, and they hugged as if they'd never stop.

"I couldn't conceive of the idea that I'd have the chance to hold you again," murmured Tammie Dean, tears streaming down her soft cheeks.

Holly said, "I'm so happy to finally meet you."

There were more hugs and tender tears. While Slade

felt a little like a voyeur, it made his heart glad to see Tammie Dean's smile through those tears, despite his reservations.

Since the stroke, she'd been pale and drawn. Now, however, she was animated and color returned to her face.

Tammie Dean stroked Holly's cheek. "You've got your grandpa's eyes."

From where he stood propping up the doorframe with his shoulder, he found it thoroughly amusing watching her with Holly. They looked more like mother and daughter than Tammie Dean did with her own daughter, Bridget. Tammie Dean's hair had streaks of grey running through it, yet the soft waves were repeated in Holly's golden hair. Their smiles were almost identical, wholesome and blissful.

His stomach wrenched.

If Holly did one thing to take away the older woman's joy, Slade would see to it that she would never have the opportunity to do it again.

Oh sure, Holly appeared to be as happy as Tammie Dean, but appearances could be deceiving. He'd learned that the hard way.

Glancing at the clock, he saw that visiting hour was almost over. "You'll have to continue your reunion tomorrow."

Holly nodded and looked toward him.

Tears filled those blue eyes of hers and something

warm inside him moved, like ice melting during a spring thaw.

He hated it.

CHAPTER FOUR

Holly pushed the nearly empty plate away from her. The tamales had been the best she'd ever tried despite the less than festive surroundings. The Mexican restaurant was so tiny, it was more like a closet, with only five tables situated so close to each other the waitress could barely move between them. Chipped mustard-colored paint on the walls had been camouflaged by a few prints of the Texas plains.

She and Slade were seated across from each other at a tiny table by the lone front window. She'd brushed his knees more than once in the close confines, making her far too aware of the cowboy when her thoughts should be with Tammie Dean.

Meeting her grandmother for the first time lingered in Holly's mind. They'd immediately grabbed each other in a hug so strong it filled an empty spot inside her.

Holly had known it existed, but never believed it could so quickly be filled.

Tammie Dean's hazel eyes had lit up the instant she saw Holly and her smile awakened a long dormant corner of Holly's heart.

The reality of meeting her grandmother far exceeded her dreams of being reunited with her birth family. Slade made the reunion possible and gratitude swelled inside her.

She glanced at him across the table, but his gaze was fixed above her head. If only he weren't so distant.

She studied him through her lashes. He'd been so quiet, he could be best described as tall, dark and silent. Although she had to admit he was handsome as well. She'd always been attracted to men who worked with their hands and his palms bore the calluses from hard work.

The problem was, she couldn't quite figure him out. At times he acted friendly, especially when discussing the Nelson family. At other times she saw mistrust in his eyes and she wondered what she'd done to make him feel that way. The only clear way to find out was to ask. "Have I done something wrong?"

"You mean besides clearing the place out of tortilla chips?"

She smiled. At least the man had a sense of humor. "You've been quiet, so I wondered."

"You and Tammie Dean seemed to hit it off."

"I thought so, too. She's such a wonderful woman."

Holly hadn't had the heart to demand answers from her, not while she was still healing from a stroke and her evident happiness at seeing Holly had been blatantly clear. Surely, given time, Tammie Dean would explain why Holly had been put up for adoption.

"Tammie Dean is one of a kind. When I moved down here as a kid, I felt like an outsider. She took me under her wing and as far as she was concerned, I was a full-fledged part of the Nelson family. That's not the same treatment I received from everyone."

So that was why he was so attached to Tammie Dean. It couldn't have been easy moving to Whispering Lake with his aunt and becoming part of such a large family. From his photo, he had been an adorable tot. Why would anyone have mistreated him or made him feel unwelcome?

"Tammie Dean and your father made my life tolerable. Harlan put me on my first horse." He smiled as if reliving the memory. The pleasant grin faded and his expression turned serious. "Being from the city, you won't understand how things work in the country. We may have our disagreements, but bottom line, we're close. We stick up for each other."

Holly nodded. She understood his point, but wasn't sure why he felt the need to make it. "I understand, Slade. I truly do, but I still want to know—did I do something wrong?"

"Not yet." He threw down some cash over the check on the table. His gaze met hers and his gray eyes were like a slab of granite. "But I'm warning you, I will not take it kindly if you hurt Tammie Dean."

"I have no intention of hurting her." Did he think she was callous and unappreciative? "You came and found me. For that I'm grateful. I don't understand why now you're acting like I'm out to get her."

Slade didn't answer. Instead he wordlessly rose from the table and gestured for her to follow. Apparently the conversation ended right then and there. Holly didn't push.

They made their way out of the restaurant to the parking lot. Once they got in the car, Slade continued the conversation as if there had never been a break. "You have a full life back in Fort Worth. After your father catches the bomber, you'll return and won't look back. It won't be intentional, but if Tammie Dean has bonded with you, it'll break her heart."

Holly paled. She'd thought making friends with Tammie Dean was a good thing. Even though she wasn't country raised, the two of them seemed to have a similar outlook on life. Whether she was raised on a farm or in the metropolis didn't seem to make much difference. "What makes you think that when I go home I'll forget Tammie Dean? Now that I've found my birth family, I'm determined to keep it."

"That's good to hear."

Still, she detected a hitch in his voice, an underlying disbelief perhaps.

As they drove back to the ranch, Holly glanced at

Slade nervously. It wasn't a bad thing that he was protective of Tammie Dean. She felt the same about her dad. Was Slade truly worried that she'd desert her grandmother now that she'd found her? Family was important to her, too. Why should he assume it wasn't?

People were people, raised in the city or not, and most loved their families for all their faults and foibles. Being raised in the country didn't mean they held the market on love.

She hoped she'd made that clear.

It wasn't yet dark, although the sun hung low in the sky, throwing shadows in the car. She didn't know him well enough to know whether he was preoccupied with driving or if he was upset. What little she did know about him, though, she admired.

He held respect for family and adored Tammie Dean. He had a quiet strength about him that made her feel safe when she was with him, even when he didn't appear to fully approve of her. His cool gray eyes seemed to observe more than the average person and she appreciated his gentleness.

Like her mom, his had passed away when he was young, too. Rather than letting bitterness take hold, which based on her experience was a risk, he'd made a meaningful life for himself with his new family.

As he pulled the sedan in front of the homestead cottage, he turned to her. "I'll give you the keys to this car and I'll drive my truck home. It's parked at Lucas's place."

"Are you sure you don't mind?" If she'd considered it, she'd have followed Slade to Whispering Lake in her own car. "I hate taking your car from you."

"It belongs to Tammie Dean. This way, you'll be able to go visit her without having to wait for someone to take you."

By that, she wondered if he meant himself. Hesitating before getting out of the car, she realized she would be alone at the cottage. She tamped down a flutter of panic. He wasn't abandoning her. She was a grown woman, after all. She could occupy herself. "I guess I'll be seeing you around?"

"You can count on it. Hang on a second and I'll get your door." He came around the side of the car and opened it for her.

It was thoughtful. He was a thoughtful man. "Thanks."

As they walked toward the front door, she asked, "How can I get in touch with you?"

"You'll find a phone listing beside the telephone in the kitchen. My number's there, as is Lucas's and the number for the main house."

While they'd eaten, Slade had filled her in on the various family members. Lucas was her first cousin.

Knowing she had the phone numbers was reassuring. When they reached the door, she wanted to say, "Nice to meet you," but it felt wrong, as if they'd known each other for years rather than just a day. Instead she offered her hand to shake. "Thanks again. For everything."

He paused a moment, then his large hand met hers. Energy crackled between them, like a jolt of electrical current, and she quickly pulled back her hand.

Slade's gaze locked with hers. Based on the look of astonishment on his face, he'd felt it, too. His surprise was followed by a look of longing so strong, her knees weakened.

A flush crept up her neck to her face, although she wasn't sure exactly why. It wasn't as if only she experienced the charge of electricity between them. Apparently the attraction was mutual.

Then he frowned. "Goodnight."

She opened the door to the cottage and turned, watching him walk toward the main house.

"Wait a second, Slade," she called out. "Do you want me to drive you to Lucas's place?"

He shook his head. "I need the fresh air."

Fresh air? Or was he afraid of that flare of attraction between them?

Without looking back, Slade disappeared behind a stand of mesquite trees. Had she misinterpreted the look of longing she'd seen in his eyes?

Not knowing for sure, she entered the cottage, her focus landing on the family photograph. Now that she'd met Tammie Dean, it intrigued her to see how the older woman had looked when she was nearly thirty years younger.

As Slade had mentioned, she and Tammie Dean favored each other. Holly just hoped that when she was Tammie Dean's age, she too would be brimming with good humor and charm.

Turning, Holly headed for the bedroom at the rear of the cottage. The rustic décor continued in the bedroom. The four-poster bed was made of sanded driftwood and covered in a handmade quilt. Something caught her eye and she stepped closer. Tucked among the decorative quilted pillows, a crisp white envelope bore the name "Holly Nelson."

Holly Nelson? She was Holly Brown.

Who would refer to her with the Nelson last name? Who would put a note there? She reached for it, then pulled out the slip of paper folded inside. Her hands trembled as she read the note. The printed words were few, but to the point.

Are you really who they say you are? To learn the truth, visit the Nelson Cemetery.

CHAPTER FIVE

The note unnerved Holly. Surely Slade hadn't left it, since the *they* referred to meant he and Tammie Dean. And Tammie Dean couldn't have done it, not from the hospital. So who could have left it for Holly to find?

She had to get to the bottom of it. The best way to find out the information the note hinted at was to visit the cemetery. She'd noticed the tiny cemetery about a mile up the main road when they'd driven from town after dinner.

Impending dusk meant she needed to hurry. The last thing she wanted was to be alone in a desolate graveyard after dark.

She climbed in Tammie Dean's sedan carrying a flashlight, placed it on the seat beside her, then backed onto the dirt road.

Who could have placed the note in her bedroom?

It's not like she'd locked the door when they'd left for the hospital. In the country few did, according to Slade.

Someone wanted her to look in the cemetery and, by doing so, she would learn something. Probably not something good, either. Why else leave an anonymous note?

The family cemetery was so small there couldn't be more than thirty graves. It wouldn't take long to check it out, so she hoped to be back to the cottage before long.

There wasn't a driveway—just an entrance off the rural highway. After pulling onto the shoulder, she grabbed the flashlight.

Waist-high blades of winter-tinged Johnson grass waved in front of the gated entrance. The grass had begun to yellow from the periodic frost, but it hadn't turned brown and hay-like yet.

This cemetery wasn't a place visited often, although footprints left by a recent visitor flattened sections of grass, giving the appearance of having created a pathway.

An unlocked chain held the bi-fold gate closed. Although she felt like a trespasser, she wasn't. Her kin were buried here and she belonged. With a determination borne of need, she quickly pulled the chain away from the gate, then entered. She wasn't sure where to start looking, nor did she know exactly what she was looking for.

Her light jacket did little to keep her warm in the

crisp evening breeze. She shivered.

Some of the headstones had toppled over, as if the weight of the souls was more than the ground could bear.

Nearby headstones showed dates going back to over a hundred years ago and if the hour hadn't been so late, she would have taken the time to explore more fully. Back in the far left corner, the gravestones appeared more current. She viewed some crushed grass, so it seemed that the recent visitor had been back there.

Trudging through the tall weeds on uneven ground wasn't easy. Would she get chigger bites, stickers, or worse? Were there snakes?

The grass inside the graveyard was somewhat shorter—knee-high. At times her heels sank into the earth and clumps of dry dirt flew when she lifted her feet. If she'd thought about it, she would have changed into something more appropriate before leaving the cottage. Even though her jacket covered her top half, overgrown old graveyards were not the place for a skirt and heels.

A sudden cold breeze rustled the leaves on the few mesquite trees, and waved their branches like specters. But as long as she didn't see any earthly threats like snakes or spiders, it wouldn't hinder her search.

At last she reached the area where the grass had been tromped down in front of the tallest tombstone in the cemetery. Her grandfather's name, Conrad Nelson, had been etched into the stone.

She leaned forward and touched the cool marble headstone, needing to make a connection. "Nice to meet you, Grandfather. I'm Holly. I understand my eyes are the same color as yours."

Even though this moment wasn't like those of her childhood fantasies involving meeting her birth family, it was oddly satisfying to know here lie kin and she promised herself she would return another day. Maybe even bring flowers.

Standing quietly, she allowed her emotions to ebb before continuing to explore.

To the right of his grave, further into the far corner, she found a narrow grave marked Wendy Farraday Nelson.

Her mother.

The wind picked up and whipped her hair. Blades of yellowing grass gyrated, as if dancing. Yet inside her, all was stillness.

Her mother.

Tears came unbidden to Holly's eyes and she bit her lip. "I would have loved to meet you, Mother."

She walked to the headstone and in a caress-like move, bent and pulled away some of the weeds growing in front of it. Closing her eyes, she prayed that somehow her biological mother would know she was here. "Out of all the Nelsons, you were probably the only one who truly wanted me. The fact that I'm here proves it."

The breeze died down, and Holly took it as a sign

that perhaps her mother was indeed aware.

Holly opened her eyes again, her throat tight as she read the headstone.

The date of death was Christmas Day. Holly's birthday.

Had Holly's birth killed her mother?

Holly's heart beat painfully in her chest and she bent her head, regret and guilt washed over her in waves. "I'm so sorry, Mother."

Was this what the note writer wanted her to learn? That giving birth had killed Wendy?

Wrapping an arm around her middle, Holly drew in a deep breath, unable to rid herself of the unpleasant thought. A slither sounded behind her. She jumped. Her senses went on high alert and her pulse raced.

Was it a snake? Scanning, she saw it was a small brown bird digging for insects, and her heart calmed. Turning back toward her mother's grave, she spotted a tiny headstone beside it, in the outermost corner of the cemetery.

She stepped toward it. The grave itself had been recently disturbed. Upturned earth formed a pile nearby.

She read the stone. *Holly Nelson*. Holly? Her stomach sank. The infant girl was born and died on the same day as Holly's mother. And on Holly's own birthday.

She gasped for air now, feeling lightheaded. Was she hyperventilating?

Confusion overflowed, leaving her with more unanswered questions.

Slade and Tammie Dean told her she was Holly Nelson. But if Holly had died at birth, she couldn't be.

She whimpered. Bringing a fisted palm to her mouth, she silenced it; tried not to sob.

She would not cry. Instead, she would figure this out. Either this had been her grave or it wasn't. Either she was dead or she wasn't. No. That didn't make sense.

She was Holly *Nelson* Brown, living, breathing, and hanging out in a spooky graveyard in the gathering darkness. She sucked in a steadying breath and collected her thoughts.

Was this whole thing—being found and brought to Whispering Lake—some sick, horrible joke? Someone out to hurt her or Tammie Dean?

Through the fading light, she glimpsed dull-yet-polished wood. A small coffin had been disinterred. It sat brokenly near a tree a few yards away. Glancing back at the baby's grave, it appeared that the coffin had come from there.

What on earth? She walked over and looked inside. It contained a sandbag. Nothing else.

Where were the baby's remains?

Spots formed before Holly's eyes and her head swam. Sit. She needed to get out of there before she fainted.

There was no place in the cemetery to rest. Staggering, she focused on the entrance gate, building momentum, running as fast as possible, slashing against fallen branches, briars and weeds. By the time she reached the roadway, she had to catch her breath and her legs were scratched and bleeding.

She didn't feel the sting. Nausea clenched her stomach. She felt cold, clammy, as if she was the one who'd been buried in that grave.

Climbing into the sedan, questions raced through her head. Had she been set up? Who would bury an empty coffin? Why? Who would send her to find the grave? What was the purpose? Why dig up an empty coffin? Was it so Holly would find it?

As a scary idea formed, her thoughts chilled. What could this mean?

As much as she wanted answers, what she wanted most was to go home. To Fort Worth. By the time she calmed down and her heart rate slowed to a more normal pace, the sun was beginning to set.

Pondering whether she should drive back to the cottage to collect her things first, or if she should return directly to Fort Worth, she heard a vehicle approach. She watched as a big red truck pulled up behind her.

Slade.

She groaned. He was the last person alive she wanted to see right now. The last person dead or alive. The last person period.

As he approached the sedan, she lowered her window.

"What are you doing out here?" he asked.

"I could ask you the same thing." Cold air blew into

the car. It seemed awfully convenient that he arrived just then.

"I'm on my way home."

That's right. He'd had to pick up his truck. Although it seemed like hours since she'd last seen him, not much time had actually passed. But that didn't mean he was innocent. "I have one question. Are you part of this scam?"

He looked taken aback. "What scam?"

He had to know exactly what she was talking about. "Holly Nelson died the day she was born. On Christmas Day. Just days away from twenty-five years ago."

"Oh." He leaned into the window, looking guilty. "I can explain that."

"Can you?" Her hands shook on the steering wheel. "Well, I'd sure love to hear it."

"When Tammie Dean sent you to the Browns, she buried an empty casket so no one would ask questions about what happened to you."

"Why would she do that?"

"You'll have to ask her yourself."

"I'm asking you." Her thoughts raced. Was he telling her the truth? If this wasn't some scam, then why hadn't he told her before? And what about the disinterred coffin? "If it's not a scam, why did someone dig up the grave?"

He stepped back, obviously surprised. "What?"

"Someone dug up my coffin."

His jaw set. "I'll be right back."

She rolled up her window, trying to find some warmth.

He marched into the cemetery, and she debated whether to leave. She wanted that explanation and to hear what he would say about the grave, so she elected to wait.

When he returned he said, "You're right. I don't know who would have done that."

"Don't you think you owe me a better explanation than that?"

"It's not my place. Can't you simply trust me that there is a good reason?"

She crossed her arms. "I don't know why I should trust you."

"I guess I deserve that." He pushed back his Stetson. "I figured it was Tammie Dean's story to tell."

Casting a glance back at the cemetery, he added, "Guess I was wrong. But now isn't the time."

"It's the only time." She had to convince him. "If you won't talk to me, I'm going home to Fort Worth. There may be a bomber, but at least my dad looks after my best interests."

His focus returned to her. "That's not an option and you know it. If you'll wait until Tammie Dean gets out of—"

"I'm not waiting."

"I knew you were stubborn." He shook his head, but she could tell there was no heat in it. "Fine. I'll tell you what I can. But not here. Let's get you out of the cold."

CHAPTER SIX

Slade could expound all he wanted that he had good reasons not to explain what was going on, but she wasn't having any of it. Holly stared into his gray eyes and for the life of her, she didn't find any hint of deceit. She would have her answers. "Meet me at the cottage, but be prepared to start talking."

Turning the car, she headed back to the cottage with Slade following. He caught up with her as she exited the car.

"You're hurt."

Of course she was. Who wouldn't be when they'd been deceived? She started to give him a snarky answer, but he was looking down at her legs. She glanced down and the instant she saw the scratches they decided to sting. "I hadn't noticed until now."

"Can you walk okay?" He lifted his arms.

"Don't even think about carrying me. I'm fine." She

hobbled for the cottage door with him right behind. "Really. I'm fine."

"I'll get the first aid kit. Take a seat on the sofa."

By the stubborn set of his jaw, he wasn't going to take no for an answer. She sat on the sofa that claimed a large amount of space in the cozy living area and waited for him to get back.

While she waited, she took note of her surroundings, from the wood-paneled walls of the living room to the worn area rugs leading to the bedroom and bath at the rear of the cottage.

A tiny kitchenette and seating area comprised the opposite corner of the room. She hadn't been upstairs yet, but presumed there was another bedroom or two on that floor, and perhaps another bath.

She grimaced. The main thing she noticed was a lack—a total absence of anything Christmas. That nook over there would be perfect for a tree. And the open staircase railing would be gorgeous covered in greenery.

Long before she had the chance to finish mentally decking out the cottage with holiday decor, Slade emerged from the bathroom with a small first aid kit and a damp washcloth. "This oughta fix you right up."

She reached out to take the items, but he shook his head. "Let me."

Her eyes narrowed. "You're just trying to buy time so you can think up a reasonable story for why you're trying to pass me off for a dead girl."

A light of amusement entered his eyes. "You think?"

"Definitely."

"Tell you what." His gaze met hers and again that jolt of attraction she'd experienced earlier hit her hard.

He said, "You sit still while I treat your cuts and I'll tell you what I can."

She noticed the note she'd received, laying where she'd placed it on the coffee table. She didn't trust him enough to enlighten him about it. Someone was looking after her and it most likely wasn't him. She surely didn't want anything or anyone to silence her unknown guardian. While he was busy tending to her scratches, she would hide the note. "Fine. Just don't hurt me."

"I won't." What he did do, though, surprised her. He knelt beside the sofa and softly, tenderly, touched one of the cuts with the damp cloth. She'd expected such a large rugged man to be anything but gentle.

And then the emotions that played over his face amazed her even further. Almost like he was afraid to touch someone too vulnerable.

"Go ahead." She drew in a ragged breath. How troubling that she found him appealing, especially when she didn't trust him. "I won't break."

He dropped his gaze and moved to the next scratch. That was her moment to act. She snuck out a hand and covered the note. As he tended to her injuries, she brought the paper up behind her head, then slid it beneath the sofa cushion.

"I hope this won't sting too bad," he said.

Had he seen what she'd done? She didn't think so.

Then she noticed the bottle of rubbing alcohol he held. "That will definitely hurt. Isn't there some antibiotic cream you could use instead?"

"If you want to chance an infection."

She gave him the disapproving look she shot at her school kids when they misbehaved. "It's a calculated risk, but one I'm willing to take."

He grinned and fumbled in the first aid kit, then came up with a tube of ointment. "This should do it."

As he applied the ointment, Holly resented the fact he could make something so mundane feel so—intimate. His touch set her nerve endings trembling. She took a steadying breath. It was totally unfair that he could so easily distract her.

Leaning up on an elbow, she snatched the tube from him with her free hand. "I'll do this. You keep your part of the bargain."

He looked up at her, his eyes heavy, hooded.

"Bargain?" he asked, obviously distracted too.

She pushed back her response to him and stayed on point.

"Start talking, bub." She pulled herself into a sitting position with her knees bent in front of her. "After seeing my grave dug up, you don't really expect me to wait until Tammie Dean is recovered, do you?"

Slade hated the fact that Holly's blue eyes were clouded with concern. He was the one who'd brought her here and he was responsible for her. He slid onto the far end of the sofa beside her feet and prepared to do the one thing he didn't want to do—talk about this with Holly. "I avoided telling you about what happened because it's troubling. Tammie Dean will handle this much better—"

"She's ill. Besides, you gave your word to look after me."

He had given his word to her dad. He'd never expected to bring Holly to Whispering Lake to find that someone had dug up the grave. He nodded, then touched her hand.

It was a battle, fighting the impulse to hold her hand. To hold her. He shook his head. He wasn't going down that road. Getting involved with a girl like her would not be smart.

And no one had ever taken him to be a stupid man.

Despite knowing better than to get involved with her, he couldn't believe how protective he felt. It had nothing to do with the fact he'd promised her dad he would look after her. The last thing he wanted to do was broadside her with more bad news, but there was no easy way to explain the situation. Once he got this off his chest, he could go about his business, return to his ranch and leave a wide berth between him and Holly Nelson Brown. "Wendy Farraday's father beat her and came close to killing her when he learned she was pregnant."

Holly went pale and brought a hand to her mouth as if she was holding back a sob. "Her *father* did that?"

"Your—grandfather—wasn't happy that she'd gotten pregnant. When she managed to escape, she ran to your father. He took her home to Tammie Dean, who insisted on a wedding."

"That doesn't explain the grave."

Slade cleared his throat, aching for Holly. Knowing that she needed to know what happened, but fully aware of how much it would hurt her. "After the wedding, your father ran off. He wrote the family a letter, explaining he was working an oilrig in the gulf. That was the last time anyone heard from him."

He watched Holly carefully, to make sure he should go on. She'd given up all pretext of dressing her wounds and nodded at him to continue.

"We recently learned he was killed years ago in San Antonio, but we didn't know that at the time. Probably shortly after he disappeared. Your grandfather was seriously ill and Tammie Dean had her hands full with taking care of the ranch, a sick husband, three younger kids and a pregnant daughter-in-law."

"I'm sure it was hard on her."

"Extremely." Slade was fully aware he hadn't reached the worst part of the story yet, but maybe he'd told her enough to fulfill her curiosity. Needing to put some distance between them, he rose to his feet. "I need something to drink. There should be some soda in the refrigerator. Want one?"

"Please."

With only a few steps from the sofa to the kitchenette, he returned with two cans of soda in moments. He handed Holly hers, then took the ointment from her and began applying it.

"You were saying?" She bobbed her soda can toward him, signaling him to go on.

"You haven't heard enough already?"

"Nothing less than the full truth will satisfy me."

She had him there. He'd gone this far and she deserved to know the truth. "Wendy's father came to the house several times, demanding money. He insisted Tammie Dean should buy his daughter and her future child." A frown creased his forehead and he paused. "He's not a nice man, Holly."

"He's still alive?"

Holly's skin had the feel of silk beneath his touch and concentrating on the events proved difficult, but he forced himself to continue. "Lives over in Avoca. I'd recommend you make it a point *not* to meet him. He's meaner than an angry rattler and just as dangerous."

Her eyes grew large, but she nodded her agreement. "I think I'm beginning to understand the problems Tammie Dean faced when my mother died."

Nothing slow about Holly. She caught on quickly. "Wendy made Tammie Dean promise not to let her father anywhere near you. Ever. But with the demands for money, your grandmother knew the brute would try to get custody as a means of forcing her hand, and her hands were already overflowing with problems. During Wendy's final days before delivering you, the doctor said her days were numbered and Wendy wouldn't live to raise you herself. Tammie Dean didn't have the ability or the energy to raise a baby, not with everything else going on. Because your father had disappeared, she looked for a good family who would love you and look after you. Your parents fit the bill."

"She made an excellent choice. I've had a good life." Holly pulled her knees to her chest. "And the grave?"

He picked up his soda and took a cool sip. "She talked it over with Conrad and they let everyone, even their own kids, believe you had passed away with Wendy. It was the only way Tammie Dean knew to keep you away from Wendy's father. An empty coffin with your name on it was buried beside Wendy's. No telling who Conrad had to pay off to make that happen. Even ailing, he was extremely powerful around these parts."

One grandfather evil and the other protective and very, very good. "How did you learn about this?"

"After Tammie Dean's stroke, when she asked me to bring you to her. She didn't have a choice. Everyone thought she'd suffered brain damage when she asked for her dead grandchild." He'd been the one to tell the others because Tammie Dean hadn't been physically or emotionally up to the task. "Do you understand why I didn't feel free to tell you sooner?"

She nodded. "But who would dig up the grave?"

"I don't have a clue. I haven't heard anything about teens digging up graves, but I suppose it could have happened."

"I'm glad you told me even though it's not what I wanted to hear. Now I have a better idea of what I'm dealing with." She sighed.

He wondered if he'd done the right thing in telling her about her background. Tammie Dean would have been extremely upset, though, if Holly had left because he wouldn't tell her everything. He'd had no choice.

"In the interests of being fully truthful, there's something I need to tell you about, too." She wouldn't look at him directly and he wondered what it could be.

She hesitated, tilting her head as if making a decision, then reached behind her head and pulled out a sheet of paper from the cushions. "When we came back from dinner this evening, I found this."

He quickly scanned the note and his lips narrowed. Why would someone do such a twisted thing? "Any idea who wrote it?"

"No. I was hoping you'd know. I found it—on my bed."

The voice that had warned him it would be a mistake to bring Holly to the Nelson Ranch returned with a crescendo of inner jolts. Maybe it was a fore-warning that she was *in* trouble rather than the other way around. "I don't like the thought of someone sneaking into the cottage and planting this. Why didn't you tell me about it before?"

She lowered her head, unable to meet his eyes. "I wasn't sure if I could trust you."

He wasn't sure if he should ask, but he couldn't help himself. "And now you're sure?"

She raised her chin. "Absolutely."

The single word wrapped its way around his heart. "I will *absolutely* do my best to live up to your trust."

"I'm banking on it."

The responsibility surprisingly settled lightly on his shoulders. How hard could it be to find out who wrote the note and why?

Weariness claimed Holly, both mentally and physically. Slade departed shortly after their talk and Holly felt reassured. There was no reason to doubt she was Tammie Dean's granddaughter. Someone resented her coming to Whispering Lake and hoped to drive her away. That was the best explanation she and Slade could come up with.

It's a good thing she wasn't so easily discouraged.

After a short phone call to check on her father, Holly was reassured about him. She changed into her nightclothes, turned on a small reading light, and went to bed with a fun romantic comedy novel. After the drama of the day, she needed some light entertainment to take her mind off things.

Her lids grew heavy, sleep tugged at her, and won.

Thunk.

The odd noise woke her from a heavy slumber.

Another thud sounded. Close. Just outside her bedroom window.

The glass shattered.

Shards sprayed, tapping the floor, the sheets on her bed.

She bolted upright, then rolled onto her feet.

In the same instant, the draperies burst into a column of flame.

CHAPTER SEVEN

After dropping Holly off at the cottage, Slade headed directly to the main ranch. He hadn't wanted to increase her anxiety, but the empty grave worried him tremendously.

Although the idea someone dug up the grave was plenty worrisome, it was the motivation for it and the note that did a number on his inner thoughts.

Who would do such a thing?

Maybe Lucas knew something. As one of Aunt Bridget and Uncle Jameson's sons and the Nelson Ranch manager, he had his fingers in most of the pies going on not only at the ranch, but also throughout Whispering Lake. Between his oversight at the ranch and his brother, Max, who was county sheriff, Lucas was the most likely person to know something about the cemetery and whether any stranger had been seen there recently.

When Slade told Lucas about the grave, he was just as concerned as Slade. He immediately called his brother and asked him to join them.

A frozen pizza and three beers later, they'd discussed all of the possibilities—that the grave had been dug up by a family member, that someone in the family had told someone else who dug up the grave, and that it might be coincidence, though none of them believed it.

"I'll put out some feelers to see if anyone saw anything," said Max as he headed for the door.

"I'd appreciate it," said Slade, grabbing his Stetson and getting ready to leave as well.

Lucas walked them to the door. "I'll check with the ranch hands and let you know if I learn anything."

Slade was the first to step onto the long porch outside the front door. Was that smoke? He sniffed the air, but wasn't sure. "Do you guys smell smoke?"

Max pointed toward the guesthouse. "Look."

Through the trees, Slade could just make out light where there should be darkness. An orange glow, where there should be blackness.

A fire smoldered at the cottage. Without a second thought, he dashed for the guesthouse. "Holly."

By the time he reached the cottage, Max pulled up with his cruiser. "Lucas is getting the fire wagon, but I've got an extinguisher."

The side of the house where Holly would sleep was ablaze. Slade darted inside, intent on saving her. As he reached her bedroom, through the smoke he made out her silhouette. She was flinging a quilt at the window, obviously trying to put out the fire.

"Forget it, Holly. You have to get out of here." He threw his arms around her to pull her from the room.

She struggled against him. "I'm smothering the flames, you idiot. Let me go."

"In another couple minutes, you'll pass out from smoke inhalation." He whipped her up into his arms and carried her from the cottage.

As they left the building and she saw the growing flames, she stopped struggling. "I hadn't realized how much smoke and fire there was."

"At least I wasn't so much of an idiot as to leave you inside."

"Thanks for getting me out." She pushed against his chest.

"What?"

"You can put me down now."

"Oh." He had to admire the way she felt pretty darn good in his arms. He reluctantly lowered her feet to touch the ground. "Sorry. Are you able to stand okay?"

"I'm fine." She coughed a little. "Now."

Slade turned to join Lucas and Max in fighting the fire. Lucas sprayed the side of the building with water coming from a fire wagon while Max emptied his fire extinguisher on the bedroom window.

A few minutes later, the fires appeared to be out, but Lucas kept spraying, "Just to be sure."

CHAPTER EIGHT

Relief coursed through Holly when Max handed her the suitcase she'd brought with her from Fort Worth. The bag was a little worse for the dampness and smoke damage, but considering what it had been through, it was in very good shape.

Slade glanced at the case in her hand. "It's a good thing you hadn't unpacked yet."

"True." As Holly glanced at the water-soaked and no longer smoking scene, anger filled her. Through clenched teeth she said, "Whoever did this was targeting me."

Slade appeared to be shocked. "What do you mean, whoever?"

"Someone set this fire when they knew I was in the bed and had turned out the lights. If I hadn't heard the breaking glass, I doubt you would have been able to arrive in time to get me out."

"So, this wasn't an accident. You're saying it was deliberate."

"Absolutely."

"Lucas," he called. "Get over here."

Lucas wiped soot from his face as he approached.

Slade said, "Holly says this was arson. Someone set the fire knowing she was there."

"Attempted murder?" asked Lucas, eyes wide.

Max nodded, all business. "Should we take Holly to the main ranch?"

"No. She's going to come stay with me," replied Slade. "It's the only way I can be sure of her safety."

"Good thinking."

Soon Holly was seated in Tammie Dean's vehicle again, with Slade behind the wheel. The drive to Slade's ranch was completed in uncomfortable silence. Slade because of fears about Holly's safety. Holly because she was too aware of how close she'd come to great injury or worse.

Minutes later, Slade dropped Holly's suitcase outside his guestroom door. "Make yourself at home."

Holly nodded, looking for all the world as if she were totally wiped out. She probably was. "Don't you think we should talk?"

"Yeah, we should." He gently nudged her into the bedroom. "After you've had some rest."

"I'm not sure I can."

"Millie's heating you up some milk. That'll help you sleep."

"Millie?"

"My housekeeper. She lives in. I called her before we came and asked her to ready your room."

When Holly nodded again, she swayed and Slade reached over to keep her from toppling.

Just then Millie came forward with a steaming mug in her hands. The older woman was exceptionally spry and didn't seem the least bit tired. "Let me set this down and I'll help Holly get ready for bed."

Slade let out a huge sigh of relief. He didn't think he could help Holly change out of her smoke-infused clothes without getting distracted in all the wrong ways. He stepped out the door. "I'll see you in the morning."

"Night," murmured Holly.

With that, he headed for the safety of his downstairs master bedroom, far away from any temptation. But unfortunately he was accompanied as he descended the stairs. Worry weighed heavily on his shoulders.

How was he going to protect Holly?

Who in the Nelson household could possibly want to harm her? Was the arsonist someone here or someone from Holly's home?

It was enough to twist his gut worrying and zigzagging, trying to discern the answers.

CHAPTER NINE

When Holly awoke the next morning, her teeth were clenched in anger. At first she couldn't understand why, then slowly as she took in her surroundings, comprehension filled her thoughts.

She was at Slade's home.

The guesthouse on the Nelson Ranch had been torched.

And someone had sent her to the Nelson cemetery to find her own ransacked grave.

Whomever did these things, assuming it was a single agent rather than two separate people, intended to either scare her off, or failing that, to cause her bodily harm—if not worse.

Thinking it over made her even angrier than before. She wasn't going to let anyone intimidate her or make her turn tail and head back to Fort Worth. And she sure wasn't going to let anyone harm her, either.

Forewarned is forearmed.

Since she was the target of these two schemes, it gradually occurred to her that she may have been the intended victim of the bombing that had sent her away to start with. She fought off chills threatening to send her shaking.

Although she couldn't think of any reason someone would want to do away with her—was it possible?

And since the activities at the ranch indicated someone familiar with the place or intimately familiar with it, enough to gain access to the guesthouse to leave the note, then it must be a biological family member or someone close to the Nelson family who was doing this. She almost couldn't breathe at the thought.

It was certainly possible that if she returned home, the physical threats could continue since there were even odds they had begun there. Her dad could still be at risk, not because of his past as a judge, but because of her only recently discovered past as a Nelson. What were the odds it was a coincidence, and there were two separate parties at work here?

Neither way was good, and she didn't much like either choice. Thankfully, she called her dad before heading to bed last night, so there was no reason to call him now and upset him with the added stress of knowing she was no safer in Whispering Lake than in Fort Worth.

There would be time enough for that, and with any

luck, she could avoid that conversation altogether by figuring out what was going on.

Despite her anger, crystal clear knowledge came to the forefront of her thoughts. She needed to decide exactly what her next steps should be. Was she going to allow an arsonist or possible murderer to chase her away before she had a chance to really know her family, especially her grandmother?

No way.

She suspected she and Tammie Dean were destined to become close friends as well as family. Holly wanted that chance, so, she wasn't going to leave. The problem was, where could she go while Tammie Dean was still in the hospital?

Holly wanted the time with her grandmother, but she also wanted to be sure she was safe as well. What to do?

By morning, Slade had just about made up his mind to send Holly back home to Fort Worth.

Since she'd arrived in town, trouble seemed to have followed her. First the note, and the graveyard, and now the fire.

Max had called him before Slade had a chance to turn in last night, stating that it had in fact been arson. Multiple cans of accelerant had been used, and the guestroom window had been the access to the house.

Holly's bedroom.

As Slade climbed out of bed with the rising dawn, it dawned on him that by sending her home to Fort Worth, he might be sending her into even worse danger. On a scale of bad to worse, a fire as opposed to a bomb seemed the lesser of two evils. He'd promised to take care of her. And down deep inside, it pleased him in a shameful way that he wanted to take care of her. He mentally shook his head.

Holly had enough problems.

There was only one real solution. His lips thinned in determination. It was best for her to remain right here where he could easily keep an eye on her. He had to convince her to stay at *his* ranch. It was safer than her living alone anywhere on the Nelson Ranch. His place was more difficult to get to plus anyone coming here would be easily seen. There would be no more sneak attacks.

And it would be more secure than her going back home where she'd been a target of a particularly malicious bombing.

Slade's place was the safest for her.

Especially since he had electronic cameras set in various positions around his place, just as a precaution, since he was quite often over at the Nelson Ranch rather than at his own place. Installing the security had made good sense to him at the time, to discourage strangers from wandering the place, and now it made even more sense.

Perhaps if Holly knew about the security she would be more willing to stay put?

He pulled on his jeans and headed into the kitchen to make some coffee, but was surprised to discover that Holly was already there. Coffee maker parts lay strewn across the counter and Holly had her head bent and almost inside the coffee maker itself.

"Looking for the IV port?"

She jumped and knocked her head against the kitchen cabinet. "Ouch." She rubbed her noggin. "An IV is a great idea. Caffeine directly to the arteries. Where do I get one?"

"Didn't mean to startle you." He chuckled, then the laughter faded as he looked at the various parts on the countertop. "Seriously, um, do you need help?"

"I was trying to figure out how to make this thing produce coffee, but apparently it's above my grade-level."

"It is a little complicated. Take a seat and I'll get the caffeine started."

She pulled out a kitchen chair and seated herself at the sixties-style Formica table, while he made the coffee.

Once he set it up, he took the seat beside her. "It shouldn't be long now."

He looked at her messed up hair, and it was kinda cute all squashed like that. "Are you one of those people who can't converse until they've had a cup or more of coffee?"

"No-o. Why would you ask that?"

He glanced down at her robe. It was the kind with buttons, but she'd buttoned it wrong and it, too, was all squashed up. "Well, are you one of those folk who can't think without caffeine?"

"No." She sounded a little huffy.

He scratched his head.

"In that case, were you in a particular hurry this morning?"

She shook her head. "What are you not saying?" She sounded aggravated with him.

But he just didn't get it. Ever since he'd met her, she'd seemed more organized than most of the people he knew. More together. She was a schoolteacher. They were usually like that, but she seemed to surpass even their abilities to keep things in order. Until now. He couldn't help himself, as he eyed her hair some more. He burst out laughing.

Exasperated, she jumped from her chair. "What?"

He rose and took her gently by the shoulders and directed her to the dining room, where there was a mirror. "Look."

She looked into the mirror, and her eyes widened. A blush traveled from her neck up to her face. "Why didn't you say something?"

"I wasn't sure if it was how you usually appear in the morning, so ..."

"Would you pour me a cup of coffee, please? I take

cream and sugar. I'll be back in a jiff." She turned and almost ran from the room.

Slade's smile was so wide that it almost hurt, but he was determined not to laugh at her again. She wouldn't take it well, and he wanted her happy and friendly when he told her she wasn't going anywhere if he had anything to say about it.

He had no plans to drive her back to Fort Worth, and he doubted there was an Uber driver willing to make such a long trip—or to mess with the Nelson's in such a way.

CHAPTER TEN

Why did Slade have such an uncomfortable look on his face? Surely she hadn't hurt his coffeemaker, but maybe he had a thing about his "things."

Holly couldn't figure it out, but as she took the last sip from her cup, she blurted, "Are you mad at me? I mean, I'm sorry I disassembled your coffeemaker—"

Slade cut her off with a shake of his head. "Why would anyone be upset about that? You're welcome to take apart any of my small appliances – and if you really want to, you can take on a large appliance, too. Just don't let all the ice melt—if you decide on the refrigerator."

Holly grinned. "I have no evil designs on any of your appliances, as long as they work."

He still remained—

Distracted?

Concerned?

Angry?

Her forefinger worried the placemat in front of her at the table. "So, why do you seem—upset?"

"Upset? Me?" He looked at her through widened eyes as he stood beside her.

"Yeah. Granted we haven't spent that much time together, but it's been enough to give me an idea of how you react, and you're reacting strangely now."

"Cards on the table?"

"Absolutely. We don't know each other well enough to be anything other than completely honest."

He exhaled, and it sounded like the waving of a white flag. He was giving up. Giving in. "I don't think you should go back home to Fort Worth."

Now that startled her. Had he come to the same conclusions as she had? "Why do you think that?"

Again with the weird expression on his face. He and his cousins couldn't have been the arsonist since they were together, and one was law enforcement. It was extremely unlikely. Maybe the expression meant Slade was trying to be gentle with her? Or trying to keep from worrying her?

"Well, Tammie Dean—"

Holly cut him off. "I thought you promised cards on the table?"

He let out a sigh, then nodded. "All right. You're right. It's just—I don't like the idea of worrying you, of scaring you."

"Believe me, I'm probably already more worried and afraid than you know."

Another sigh. "I'm worried the bombing at your dad's place wasn't directed at him."

"Granted. I may have been the target."

"You already figured that out?"

"It seems logical, given the fact there was another attempt on my life last night."

He remained silent, studying her from head to toe. "You don't appear to be freaked out over it."

"I try to limit freaking out to an internal reaction." She shot him a nervous grin. "Of course I'm worried."

He nodded.

"But I'm also determined."

Again he nodded.

"And angry down to the bottom of my toes."

"Now that's a reaction I can endorse," he said. "I didn't expect it, but now that I think on it, it's the best determination you could have reached."

"Thank you kindly, sir." She turned serious again. "Now, I do want to remain safe, but ... I want to catch the scoundrel trying to take me out, and not caring who else he harms in the process."

"He? You're saying it was a man? Did you see him?"

She shook her head. "No. It was just a figure of speech. It could have been a woman or a man or both, or a bobcat, even, except they probably don't have much of a throwing arm and their note-writing skills are practically nonexistent."

She glanced down at her hands, then back up at him. She was trying to be lighthearted in an effort not to worry him further. However, the memory was too fresh, and definitely robbed her of strength as she admitted how vulnerable she'd been. "I didn't see anyone. I just heard the sound of the cans of accelerant bursting through the bedroom windows."

"I hate the fact this happened to you, Holly." His voice shook with emotion. "Even more, I hate that this happened to you on my watch. I promised your father. I was responsible for you then, and I am even more responsible for you now."

"You couldn't have known."

"Now I do." His chin stiffened with steely determination.

CHAPTER ELEVEN

At the sound of Millie's voice coming toward them from the staircase, Holly and Slade silenced.

Slade pulled out a chair at the kitchen table and took a seat. Millie always objected to him hovering, and he hadn't meant to do it. But his discussion with Holly was discombobulating at best, and downright fearsome at worst.

"Good morning," greeted Millie as she entered the kitchen. "Glad to see you're both up with the hens."

"Mornin', Millie," said Slade.

"Good Morning," said Holly cheerfully.

"I see you've got coffee already, too." Millie opened the side-by-side refrigerator door and spoke with her head buried inside. "I'll have your breakfast ready in a jiff."

"Oh, no," cried Holly. "I couldn't put you out that way. I'll get my own."

"Oh, no, you won't. It's my job, and frankly, you'd only get in my way." She pulled out a carton of eggs and a butter dish, then closed the refrigerator. "So how do you like yours?"

"Scrambled, please," Holly said meekly. Slade wondered what Millie's trick was to get Holly so complaisant.

"Bacon or sausage?"

"Just some toast, please."

Wow. Millie was certainly impressive.

"You want your usual, Slade?"

"Yes, ma'am."

"Why don't you take your newspaper and go sit out on the porch while us two ladies chat and get to know each other."

That wasn't a question. She'd given him his marching orders. Slade got up to go, but just then the phone rang. He waited while Millie picked up the receiver.

"Hello," she said. Followed by a head nod and a "Yes'm."

She held the receiver out to Slade. "It's Tammie Dean."

Slade took the receiver she held out to him and answered. "Mornin', Tammie Dean."

It only took him a few minutes to disconnect the call. He turned to Holly and smiled widely, fully aware they'd heard at least *his* side of the conversation. "After lunch today I'm heading over to the hospital and bringing your grandmother home. Want to ride along with me?"

"Oh, you bet." Holly's heart skipped with joy. "Where are we taking her?"

"Home."

"To the main ranch?"

"That's her home."

"She lives there alone?"

"She has been."

"Well, she's not going to do it anymore. I'm moving there with her." Holly stood. "I'm going to pack."

"Wait a sec," Slade said, holding out his hand in a slow down gesture. "I thought we already determined you were safer here with me and Millie—"

"That was before we learned Tammie Dean is coming home. She's going to need some help, and I'm just the person to give it."

"I don't doubt you'd be very good at helping her out, Holly. I just worry about how safe you both will be."

"We'll be perfectly fine."

"The two of you alone, and one of you recovering from a stroke? What if the arsonist returns?"

"He's not going to torch the main house."

"He could."

"Fine."

"You'll stay here?"

"No-oo. I'll get more protection for the two of us."

"A security system in only a couple of hours?"

She pointed to the clock. "There's plenty of time for what I need. The security system can come later."

CHAPTER TWELVE

"I can't believe you talked me into this."

Holly shot him a broad grin. "If I need protection, it might as well be fun protection."

"We're not talking water guns, Holl." Slade observed the sign over the entrance in front of them, then sighed. "Don't you think the Animal Rescue might be taking it too far in the wrong direction?"

She tossed her head. "I'm an animal and, according to you, I need rescuing."

"This is serious. Deathly serious."

She nodded, but his words didn't seem to have any other impact on her. It didn't take long for him to realize there was no way he was going to win this one. "I suppose a very large and very loud dog might protect you until the security system is installed. Maybe you can take out a dog loaner?"

"Don't be ridiculous," Holly said as she exited the truck. "Let's go find the perfect pooch."

At the best of times, that would be a lousy alliteration, but he did as she suggested.

Holly reached the glass door fronting the Animal Rescue before Slade caught up with her. He held it open for her to enter first.

Stepping into the building, she had expected the floor to be concrete, but instead it was an ancient wooden floor. The smell of warm dog bodies, and acridity assailed her. One glance around the room told her the ancient facility used to be a small house. Now along one wall in front of her was a counter, with two volunteers standing behind it.

"Welcome to BowWow House," said a perky volunteer, her scrunchied ponytail dancing.

The other one, who had a morose expression, said, "Can I help you find the perfect pooch?"

The way she said it made Holly wonder whether there was a funeral she hadn't heard about. Surely not. But the volunteer had mentioned a *perfect pooch*. Slade had cringed when he heard the expression, making Holly smile. "I knew this was the right place to come. Yes, please," she told the cute young volunteer, "I'd love to find my *doggy destiny*."

The sad-seeming teen giggled. "Oh, I like that one. Mind if I use it?"

Holly laughed as Slade emitted a quiet groan. "Help yourself. I'm intent on finding myself a *honey of a hound*."

She elbowed Slade and followed the girl down a long hallway.

"Are you looking for a puppy or a dog?"

"I'd prefer an adult. One who's already house broken. And I'm not specific on age."

"Great. We've got lots of darling doggies for you to choose from. Do you prefer a breed or a mutt?"

"Again, I'm easy. I just want to find the right dog—for me." She thought about it as they entered an outdoor area lined with pens. "Oh, and I'd prefer one who barks."

The volunteer stopped in her tracks and looked back at her. "What?"

"I like a dog who barks."

"That's what I thought you said, but I couldn't believe it. Most people want quiet dogs."

"I just want a happy one."

"Oh, in that case, I have exactly the right dog for you. Even his name is perfect. He's called Lobo."

"I'm intrigued," Holly said.

"Right this way." The volunteer stopped in front of a pen. Inside was a small, fluffy white pooch. Almost a toy poodle in size, but although there was a resemblance to a poodle, the dog didn't seem to be one. "I can see how the name fits."

He had a huge wolfish grin on his face.

"What kind of dog is he?" Holly laughed and asked over Lobo's frantic yips of joy.

"Maltese."

She hadn't heard of the breed before, although she'd seen an animal like him previously. "Can I pet him?"

"Of course." The volunteer swung the chain link gate open.

Slade spluttered. "You've got to be kidding."

"What?"

"I thought you were looking for a large dog."

"Or a loud dog and, judging by Lobo's barks, he's quite a loud doggie," Holly bent and scooped Lobo into her arms, "Aren't you sweetheart?"

Lobo instantly silenced and gave Holly's cheek a friendly lick.

"Guard dog." Slade snapped his fingers twice and his voice lowered. "A protector."

That was enough to annoy Lobo, who began barking loudly again. Specifically at him.

"See?" Holly cried. "He's a fabulous guard dog. Listen to him bark!"

His expression said he preferred dogs who were seen and not heard. "I'm not the bad guy."

"My point exactly." She grinned at him. "Just imagine how Lobo will bark at someone with evil intentions."

She kissed the top of his white floppy haired head.

"You're exactly the right guard dog for me, aren't you, Lobo?"

Lobo barked and licked her again.

Holly met the volunteer's gaze. "I'll take him."

"Can't we at least look at a few other dogs? A dog large enough to scare off someone who even considers doing something wrong?"

If she hadn't known better, she would have thought Slade was whining.

"I just know Lobo is the right dog for me, Slade. When you know, you know."

"I can only imagine the ranch hands' reaction to me bringing home a tiny poodle."

"She's not a poodle," said both Holly and the volunteer in unison.

"And you're not the one bringing her home. I am." Holly hugged the dog to her chest and met her dog's gaze. "You and I are going to be best friends, aren't we, Lobo?"

The dog yipped.

Slade shook his head sadly. "I don't know how much protection he'll be for you and Tammie Dean. Have you thought of that?"

"Yes. You're installing security and until then, we'll have our early warning system, won't we, Lobokins?"

He sighed. "I have a bad feeling about this."

"You'll have to trust me this time, Slade. I'm going to rescue Lobo and in return, he's going to rescue me. You'll see."

"Maybe so. At any rate, he's the perfect tiny size to fit in a stocking over the fireplace."

"Are you my Christmas doggie?" she asked the pup, who wriggled happily. Holly knew she couldn't find a better dog to both keep her company and help keep her safe.

"He is." Slade eyed the volunteer. "I'm covering the adoption fee."

CHAPTER THIRTEEN

When they arrived at the hospital to collect her grandmother, Holly and Lobo waited in a small park nearby.

Lobo darted between bushes, chasing leaves while Holly took a seat on a park bench. Lobo found a branch and started to run off, so Holly jumped up and ran after the pup.

"Come back, Lobo." She just about caught up with the dog, when Lobo dropped his stick and bristled. He turned and faced behind her at a man, and uttered a low-voiced growl in his direction.

"Lobo!"

The last thing Holly wanted was for her new dog to get into a row with a strange man.

She grabbed up her new dog, and said, "Shush."

Then she looked up at the man. He remained about

20 feet distant, and the more she looked at him, the stranger he seemed.

He was older, and dressed in a plaid shirt and jeans. He simply stood in place, staring at both Holly and the dog.

It wasn't a friendly stare, but it wasn't quite a glare, either. She didn't know quite how to interpret it.

She opened her mouth to apologize for her dog, she saw that Slade was coming back to the truck. The man abruptly turned and left. Holly called after him, "Sorry," but the stranger didn't react.

Lobo and she took seats in the back as Slade slid into the driver's seat of the truck. He then turned the truck to the hospital pick-up entrance to get Tammie Dean. Once Slade got the older woman situated in the front, Holly asked if Slade had seen the man at the park.

He shook his head. "I was concentrating on Tammie Dean and didn't notice anything. Did anything happen?"

"Not really. I was just curious." Holly directed her attention to her grandmother. "I'm so glad you're coming home, Tammie Dean. I'm going to stay with you and help with whatever you might need."

"That's wonderful." She held out her hand for Lobo to sniff. "Now, who is this sweet baby?"

Slade groaned, apparently aware Lobo had captured another female heart.

By the time they arrived back at the main ranch, Holly, Lobo and Tammie Dean had already established a promising and satisfying friendship. Although the older woman was a little weak, she was in great spirits, and her underlying color was excellent.

From the paperwork sent home from the hospital, Tammie Dean was to take it easy for a few days, but after that she should be ready to return to her normal routine with no need for physical therapy. Obviously, the stroke had been relatively minor and was more of a warning rather than a major stroke.

With her new medications, and a better diet, Tammie Dean could live for another half century. She was so sweet and friendly, Holly couldn't help but be thrilled that at least one member of her biological family was someone she could easily love and who already seemed to love her. Taking care of her would be a delight and a treat.

While Slade helped to get Tammie Dean settled on the sofa in the living room, Holly had taken Lobo out to do his business. When she returned, it was to find that her suitcase had been taken to an upstairs bedroom, while Tammie Dean explained that her own sleeping quarters would be moved to a spare downstairs room.

"What items do you need for me to bring you from upstairs? A house robe?" Holly asked.

"I've made a little list. It's not long," Tammie Dean said, then dug in her handbag to pull out a small spiral notepad. She ripped out a page and handed it to Holly. "See?"

Holly scanned the page. "Only nine items?"

"For now at least." Tammie Dean grinned. Lobo jumped up on the sofa to join her, and Tammie Dean gave the pooch a gentle hug. "By tomorrow I might have a much longer list for you."

"It's a deal," replied Holly. "I'll go get this stuff and be back shortly."

By the time she returned to the living room, Slade was nowhere in sight. "Where is Slade?"

"He's headed off for now. It's just the three of us—you, Lobo and me. Maybe we can get cozy and talk about your life and interests. I can't wait to learn more about you."

Lobo barked and spun around, trying to get more comfy beside Tammie Dean.

"Oh, no. Get down, Lobo."

"Don't be silly. He's just fine here with me, aren't you, sweet boy?"

Lobo yipped, circled some more, then cuddled up close to Tammie Dean.

"I thought you were *my* dog," Holly said.

Lobo tilted his head and seemed to smile reassuringly. "Wolf."

Lobo wasn't really a wolf, but even he seemed to enjoy the play on words since the Spanish word for wolf was lobo. No mere "woof" for him, despite his diminutive size.

Holly took a seat beside her grandmother. "I'm so glad you like dogs."

"Used to have a slew of 'em—ranch dogs—so it's great to have Lobo here. He's extremely well behaved. How long have you had him?"

After a quick glance at her smart watch, Holly said, "About four hours."

Tammie Dean cackled with laughter. "That long?"

"Slade thought we needed some protection, so—"

"Well, I guess he thinks we need even more protection. He's ordering a security setup in the morning, and he's spending the night until it's installed."

"What? He's coming back?"

"He's picking up his gear, then getting fried chicken for us for dinner. I hope you like it?"

"Love it. I'm not a picky eater."

"Me, neither. Put it in front of me, and I'll manage to chow it down."

Holly smiled and reached over to stroke the back of Tammie Dean's soft hand. "I guess I take after you on that."

Half an hour later they were poring over an old photo album that had childhood photos of Holly's father, when Slade returned with their dinner.

They knew he was back because Lobo jumped from the sofa and raced to the front door where he waited, barking, for Slade to enter. As the door opened, Lobo barked twice at Slade, circled, then led him to the kitchen.

Her new dog certainly had his priorities straight. Food first, discussion later.

"This is my daughter, your Aunt Bridget." Tammie Dean pointed at a last photo before closing the album. "You'll meet her tomorrow."

"I'm looking forward to it. When are you expecting her?"

"First thing. As soon as she hears you moved in, she'll be here with her overnight bag."

Holly's surprise must have been visible on her face.

"Don't worry, hon. I'll send her packing. She takes after her daddy and his leadership ways."

"Leadership?" Her grandmother had totally lost her. "Do you mean she runs the ranch?"

"Absolutely not. Truth to tell, she's bossy like her Daddy. Good thing she has three boys of her own, otherwise she'd be sticking her nose into everything I do." Tammie Dean shoved off her blanket. "Now scoot. That chicken isn't getting any warmer."

CHAPTER FOURTEEN

The next morning after breakfast, Tammie Dean handed Holly a new sheet of spiral notebook paper. "This is the guest list for Christmas. I'm telling my kids and grandkids, but if you don't mind, I'd appreciate it if you would look these others up in my address book," she patted a small book beside her, "and give each of them a call to let them know the particulars. You can tell them I'm providing all of the big things, like turkey, ham and prime rib, but if they want to bring a side or two of their choice, it'll be appreciated but isn't required."

"Can do," said Holly.

"You can use the office phone if you like," added Tammie Dean. "It'll be much quieter in there. Bridget is due at any time."

Holly smiled, understanding that this was to be her

excuse to avoid Bridget as much as possible. "Okay. I'm heading to the office now."

Within minutes she was seated at the desk, and thumbing through the address book looking for Monty Joe Nelson's phone number when she heard the front door open. So did Lobo.

The dog jumped off her lap and headed for the entryway, barking and growling (as much as a little tiny dog can growl, which was surprisingly ferocious) all the way.

Holly discarded the address book and followed Lobo from the room. "Come back here, Lobo."

By the time she'd caught up with him, he had cornered a woman Holly presumed to be her aunt near the front door. Holly scooped the pooch up. "Shush, Lobo."

The older blonde shook her clothing as if the little dog had contaminated it. "About time you got him."

"Sorry."

She looked at Holly through narrowed eyes. "I suppose you're supposed to be my niece."

"I don't know what you mean by that."

Bridget gave her an assessing look up and down. "Your sweeter than candy expression fails to satisfy me. I said what I mean. I doubt you're any kin of mine."

Holly shrugged. "Doesn't matter to me whether you're satisfied or not."

Bridget opened her mouth to say something, probably even more antagonistic based on her hostile expression, but she snapped her mouth shut and quickly plastered a false smile on her face as Tammie Dean joined them.

"Hello, dear." Tammie Dean gave Bridget a little hug. "I'm so glad you could make it today."

Bridget gave Holly another once-over. "I'm glad I wasn't any later."

Tammie Dean must have been unaware of the undercurrents swirling around Bridget. "Well, you did miss breakfast. But Millie sent over some cookies. You do still love chocolate chip cookies, right?"

"You know they're my weakness."

"Mine, too," said Holly. "I love them more than just about anything."

Bridget gave her a frown. "I presume this here is Holly Brown?"

"Absolutely. Holly *Nelson* Brown. My granddaughter and your niece."

Bridget shrugged off her jacket and scarf, and hung them from the hall tree. "If you say so, Mom."

They all entered the living room, where Tammie Dean swung her feet onto the cushions beside her on the sofa.

Bridget took a seat beside the sofa.

"So, I'll get back to my phone calls," Holly said.

"Thanks, honey," said Tammie Dean.

Bridget's expression said, *Good riddance.*

Holly didn't mind in the least. She was surprised, though, by how much animosity Bridget had for her when they first met. Surely that kind of dislike should only stem from personal interactions. Not just based on the fact of her existence.

She shrugged. It took all kinds. She picked up the phone and dialed Monty Joe's number.

Slade had his marching orders. Tammie Dean said that he and Holly needed to take care of her Christmas decorations, and he was happy to help out.

He peeked in the study where Holly had been on the phone for the last several hours. "Are you about done yet?"

Holly ran her hand through her hair. "Oh, yeah. I just finished the last call to Charlie Nelson Davis. There's going to be a huge crowd here on Christmas Eve and Christmas Day."

"There always is every year. So, Tammie Dean asked if we could work on putting up her Christmas decorations. What do you say?"

Holly rose from her chair. "I say yes!"

CHAPTER FIFTEEN

Holly had lots of fun putting up the Christmas decorations with Slade. Especially once Bridget had left. It had been discouraging having disapproving eyes watching her every move.

When Aunt Bridget was ready to leave, her husband Jameson Wilson came to fetch her, having dropped her off earlier.

At long last, she and Uncle Jameson were formally introduced by Slade. The middle-aged man shook her hand vigorously.

"I've met two of your sons," Holly said to the couple. "They are such nice and attractive young men."

Aunt Bridget raised her brow at that, as if she feared Holly was going to come onto one of her sons.

"They both seem very good at their jobs and I'm glad to have such resourceful relatives." Holly didn't know what else she could say to make it clear she wasn't going to chase their sons—especially since they were first cousins.

Uncle Jameson grinned widely. Wide enough to expose his back teeth. Apparently he planned to make up for Aunt Bridget's lack of friendliness.

"I suppose you know I handle all of the Nelson Ranch finances," said the middle-aged man. He was a little paunchy, but not enormously so. Just enough to soften his facial features.

Holly turned to indicate Slade. "Yes, he mentioned that."

"I want you to know that I'm available whenever you need a financial advisor. Keep it all in the family, like."

"Thank you. I'm afraid that on my school teacher's salary, I don't really need money advice as much as I could use some extra cash." Holly grinned sheepishly.

"You never know how things can change," he said. "You know where to find me if you need me."

With that, he collected Bridget by her arm and led her to their car, with Holly and Slade following and giving a friendly goodbye wave.

Outside the huge main ranch house after they left, she and Slade had hung lights and garlands and wreaths and all sorts of other things. Inside they'd strung holly and more garlands and more decorations. Lastly, they were now working on the Christmas tree.

Slade handed her a beautiful red ornament. It was

trimmed with white sparkles and flashed in the lights adorning the tree.

"Oh, I really like this one." It was a beautiful and glittery blue and satiny white, full-length glass Santa Claus ornament.

"That one is from when Tammie Dean was a girl. So many of these ornaments are true antiques, and all are family heirlooms, collectables or hand-me-downs. Tammie Dean usually buys a new box each year, but this year she hasn't had time."

"Maybe we could do that sometime tomorrow?"

"We can go into town and see what selection they have left."

"Perfect." And speaking of perfect, Holly found the exact spot to hang the ornament.

Slade handed her another ornament. This one was a deep blue, in a cylindrical shape, and touched with what looked like melting golden wax. "Nice."

"You sure make hanging these ornaments more fun, Holly. I'm enjoying seeing them fresh through your eyes."

Holly's did her best to imagine her eyes twinkling at Slade. "Thank you, kind sir. No one ever said my eyes were fresh before."

He tilted his head at her. "I meant that as a compliment."

Holly bumped his shoulder with hers. "Don't be silly. I knew what you meant."

"In that case, now that you mention it, not only your eyes look fresh, but so do your lips." He lowered his head and she thought it was to kiss her, but he immediately drew back at the sound of someone entering the room.

"Having fun putting up the bulbs?" asked Tammie Dean. She looked very good for having recently come home from the hospital. In fact, Holly thought she looked extremely perky. And too innocent—like she knew she'd interrupted their almost-kiss.

Holly wished her grandmother had been a few minutes later. Had Slade been about to kiss her? She thought so. She hoped so. She wanted to know for sure he had intended to kiss her—because she *certainly* would have enjoyed that kiss.

"You're a real taskmaster," replied Slade to Tammy Dean. "You've got us doing your bidding, oh wise one."

Her grandmother grinned. "Don't make me give you a whippin'. I'm not too feeble to do it, you know."

"You may not be too feeble, but you've never given anyone a whippin', deserved or not."

"I'm afraid that's true." Tammie Dean shook her head. "It looks as if you're just about done with the tree."

"We've finished everything else," said Holly. "And you can ignore Slade's grumping. We both have had a great time decorating the ranch. I love your family decorations."

"I'm rather attached to them myself."

"I especially love the whale ornament. It looks really old."

Tammie Dean nodded. "It was old when I was a girl."

Holly enjoyed old things—almost any type of antique. Most of her friends were all about the modern —or midcentury modern, but they generally didn't actually want something that actually dated from the midcentury. What they wanted was new pretending to be old.

She didn't get it, but was philosophical about it taking all kinds. "The angel on top is truly beautiful, too."

"That is new." Tammie Dean giggled. "Or at least to me it's new. Your biological father, Harlan, bought it for me for Christmas when he was about twelve years old."

The gorgeous angel ornament snagged Holly's gaze. "He had wonderful taste. I love it."

"As do I, my dear. As do I."

"Well, I hope you think we did a good job with the lights," said Slade, obviously fishing for a compliment because the tree was almost ablaze with all of the strings of lights.

"You did a marvelous job," Tammie Dean said. "I'm so glad you're the subject of my task mastering because you do such excellent work."

Slade added two more sparkling ornaments to the tree, then stepped back. "There. I think we may be finished."

"Except we plan to shop for some new ornaments tomorrow. Is there any special kind you'd like?"

"Yes, please. I want something pretty and sparkly."

"Anything more specific?" asked Slade.

"Not really. Every year I look for something special. Like that whale ornament you mentioned. I like ornaments that bring a memory, or speak to something meaningful. Like those little bird house ornaments."

"They're some of my favorites."

"Mine, too." Tammie Dean stepped back from the tree and admired it. "So, go find more favorites, please."

"We will do our best." Holly fought back tiredness, but her sleepy eyes won. "On that note, I think it's time for me to head to bed."

"I'm ready to turn in, too," said Tammie Dean. "In fact, that's what I came in to tell you two."

Slade turned and gave her a big hug. "Good night, Tammie Dean."

She patted him on the shoulder, then turned to Holly and wrapped her arms around her. "Good night, grandbaby. I hope you have sweet dreams."

The tight hug Tammie Dean gave her was truly special. "Let me tuck you in for the night. I'm here to help *you*, remember?"

"You've helped me so much today. I'm afraid I've been taking advantage of you."

"You couldn't possibly. Come on, let's get you ready for bed."

"Have a good sleep," added Slade.

"I'm feeling very loved and taken care of. Thank you both."

It didn't take long for Holly to get Tammie Dean settled into bed, then come upstairs to her own room.

Taking a seat on the bed, she slipped off her shoes and pulled out her smartphone.

"Hi, Dad."

"Evening, pet. I've been waiting for your call."

"You have?"

"Yes. Apparently there are somethings or at least *something* you haven't told me."

"What would that be?"

"Maybe a small mention to me about a fire might have been indicated?"

"Oh. That." Holly's heart beat fast. She wasn't used to being not completely forthright with her dad, and guilt washed over her. "You're right. How did you find out?"

"Believe me, enough people are watching over you, I received several reports today."

She should have thought of that. Her father was connected to law enforcement in ways even she couldn't fathom. "I should have said something."

"Why didn't you?"

"I'm perfectly safe now, and I didn't want to worry you."

"Oh, darling, you have worried me from the first day you were placed in my arms."

Her heart warmed and she laughed, "Well, there is that. But in this case, I didn't want you to worry more than your usual worrying quota."

"I've been doing that ever since I heard about the fire. And you didn't mention it when we last spoke."

"Everything is under control. I'm at Tammie Dean's main ranch. I have a dog, a new dog I need to tell you about named Lobo, and Slade is in the process of getting a security system installed here. In the interim, he's staying in the main ranch house, too. But I don't think there's a threat. We're taking precautions just in case."

"Good. I'm glad to hear you're all being cautious. But Holly, my heart can't handle another scare like I had when I learned there'd been a fire where you had been staying. Especially when the reports came through as suspected arson."

"It was arson. That's why we're being so careful now."

"Just as long as you are. Careful I mean. Now, about this dog—"

After she filled him in on her new best friend, and Lobo barked into the phone a few times just to let her dad know he was looking after Holly, they disconnected the call.

As she was saying goodbye, she noted a glass of milk sitting on the table beside the bed. It was cool to the touch. In addition to the glass, beading with evaporation, there was a small saucer of cookies as well. They appeared to be chocolate chip cookies with some kind of icing. They looked delicious.

She extended her hand to pick one up, but stilled. Where had the milk and cookies come from?

She knew for a fact that Tammie Dean hadn't come upstairs to deliver them, and there was no way Slade would have come into her room, much less delivered a snack without telling her first. At least she didn't think so.

She slid her shoes back on and went to her bedroom door, then entered the hallway. Unsure which of the many bedrooms was Slade's, she called out to him, and began knocking on doors. She struck gold when she knocked on the fifth door.

"What's up?" asked Slade, opening his door a crack. His hair was mussed as if he'd been lying down.

Fighting a moment of guilt, she asked, "Did you bring me milk and cookies?"

"If there were any cookies to be had, I probably would have eaten them all myself. So, no, I didn't bring you anything. Sorry."

"I'm not complaining," Holly replied, then pointed toward her bedroom. "I think you ought to take a look at the snack on my bedside table. I didn't bring it up myself, and Tammie Dean sure didn't. If you didn't bring it, then who did?"

His brows furrowed. "Lead the way."

When they reached her bedroom, Slade headed directly to her bedside table. He didn't touch the glass or saucer, but he did lean over and sniff each. "I don't smell anything out of the ordinary."

"I didn't either. Earlier today I had one of Millie's chocolate chip cookies, but they didn't have icing on top the way these cookies have."

"Hmm. I haven't seen that before."

"Neither have I seen frosted cookies, except usually sugar cookies or gingerbread. Those look to be chocolate chip."

"How can you tell?"

"Look on their sides. They aren't a consistent light color like one sees with a sugar cookie. They look like they contain chocolate chips."

"Could be." Slade pulled his phone out of his back pocket, then quickly dialed a number. "Max? I've got a situation here that you might be interested in."

He quickly informed Max, Tammie Dean's grandson and child of Bridget, about the bedside snacks. "Okay."

Slade disconnected the call. "Max is on his way over."

"What does he think?"

"Like us, he thinks it's suspicious."

Holly's vision swam and she swayed before reaching out a hand to the doorjamb to steady herself.

"Careful there. Are you okay?" asked Slade.

"I've been better." It took every ounce of her power and attention to stay in the moment and not slide off into fear. "Do you think this is another attempt on my life?"

"To be honest, I don't know what to think other than the glass of milk and those cookies didn't magically appear on your bedside table."

CHAPTER SIXTEEN

The next morning when Slade checked his phone, he saw that Max had already sent him the results from the samples of the milk and cookies.

He scanned down and saw that the milk was perfectly fine. Typical milk.

As he scanned further down, his brows drew together. The cookies, not so much typical. In fact, they contained an enormous amount of sleeping medication. He recognized the pharmaceutical name as being the same type of sleeping pill that Tammie Dean had been taking since the death of her husband.

That tore it.

He checked his recent calls and pushed the connect button on the number for the security company. "I need to speak with Brandon."

"How can I help you?" Brandon asked.

"I know you said you can't get out here to the Nelson Ranch until the end of the week, but something serious has come up. An incident. I need that security installed right away. Today if possible."

"I can't give you everything you want today, but I'll see what I can do," replied Brandon. "I should be able to at least get a basic system going tonight, and finish up the extra cameras and monitors in the next day or two."

"And signage? Can you put that up today, too?"

"You bet. That should scare most intruders away, even if we're still working on the bells and whistles."

"Thanks. I appreciate your help."

After disconnecting that call, he phoned Max.

Max said, "I'm sending a team over to dust for prints, but I don't think we'll find anything. At least we'll have something on file if anything else happens. But Slade, I'm seriously concerned about what's happening to Holly."

"You and me, both. The security company is going to start work today and they'll have a basic system in place by tonight."

"That's good. Don't you think, though, you might suggest to Holly that she take a vacation? For her health? And maybe not tell anyone where she's going?"

"Nah." Slade shook his head. "I can suggest it, and I will, but she's just as stubborn as Tammie Dean. She'll want to stay and catch whomever is doing this."

"Well, do your best to convince her, man. Her life may very well depend on it."

"You got it."

Even though Slade's ear was already feeling sore from so much time on the phone, next he called his own house. "Millie?"

"Morning, Slade. Miss me already?"

"In fact I do. Any chance I could convince you to come stay at Tammie Dean's for a few days? We could use the help with meals, and there's been an incident I need to tell you about."

"All you needed to do was ask." He could hear the sound of her footsteps as she apparently rushed to get ready. "Give me half an hour to pack a bag, and I'll drive over."

"You're a peach, Millie."

She grumbled, "I'm not a stinking fruit, young man."

"Well, you are the best." Slade hoped he'd made a decent recovery.

"See you soon. You can fill me in when I get there."

"Thanks, Mill."

Slade put his phone in his back pocket, then opened his bedroom door. The sooner he talked with Holly, the sooner he'd get it over with. He knew it wasn't going to be pleasant, but he'd promised to take care of her, and he had best step up his efforts. Like by about tenfold. It was past time for his A-game.

Only luck had saved her from both murder

attempts, no thanks to him. He had to do a much better job. His jaw clenched. He'd promised.

Reaching the kitchen, he found Holly, Lobo and Tammie Dean already huddled over the table.

"Good morning, ladies and gentleman," he said, leaning down to give Lobo a quick scratch on his head.

Tammie Dean held up her face for a brief kiss, then grabbed his hand before he stepped back. "Before you get started, Holly told me about the milk and cookies."

"That they were poisoned?"

"No." Tammie Dean met Holly's gaze. "You didn't mention poison."

"I didn't know they were." Holly's eyes were wide as she directed her gaze to him. "Slade?"

When he was out in the pasture he expected to have to watch his steps. But not inside. Not with Tammie Dean. But he'd stepped right in it. "Toxicology came back that there was sleeping medicine in the cookies."

"The cookies?"

"Probably the icing."

"So it wasn't actually poison," clarified Tammie Dean.

"No, ma'am," he replied. "Just enough sleeping medication to make sure anyone who ate them wouldn't wake up."

"Ever?" the older woman asked with a shiver.

Slade turned his eyes down, and slowly nodded.

Holly reached out a hand to keep from stumbling.

"Are you okay?" he asked, gently grabbing her shoulder.

She leaned into his support and felt a little steadier. "I'm not sure if I'll ever be truly okay again. Someone is deliberately targeting me."

"I know I haven't done a great job of looking after you—"

"I'm not blaming you." Her head swam. How does one deal with this kind of evil? "It's not your fault that someone wants me," she gulped, "—permanently out of the way."

Tammie Dean said, "What is going on? I don't understand."

"Neither do I," said Holly. Stepping back from Slade's support, she cleared her throat, rubbed her eyes, then determinedly opened them. She had to be brave and keep her wits. She couldn't allow someone to scare her anymore. "But I intend to find out."

"I'm sorry I didn't tell you earlier, Tammie Dean, but the guesthouse fire—it was deliberate and happened while Holly was in bed." Slade's jaw clenched. "We weren't positive it was intended to harm Holly, but now it sure looks that way. Max is all over it."

"I'm glad the Sheriff's Department is involved," replied the older woman. "This explains why I learned I'm getting a security system when no one asked my opinion on it."

"Surely you agree?"

"Obviously." She stared him down. "I would merely have expected to have been consulted about something affecting the life of my granddaughter as well as my property. At least, the last time I checked the Nelson Ranch belongs to me?"

"I was afraid that worry would make your condition worse."

"What makes it worse is getting me mad. And it angers me when I'm not kept informed." Tammie Dean reached out and touched Slade's arm. "You understand?"

"Yes, ma'am, I do. I'm afraid I was guilty of wanting to protect you as well as underestimating you. I won't keep things back in the future, unless you tell me otherwise, or your health condition is so poor you can't communicate. Will that do?"

"Yes. Thank you, pet." Tammie Dean turned to Holly. "Now, child, I can understand why you didn't say anything if you didn't know for sure someone was targeting you, so I'm not holding you responsible."

The stress seeped out of Holly's body, leaving her feeling much lighter, both physically and emotionally. With a grandmother like Tammie Dean, how could she fear the worst? "I'll keep you informed, too."

"See that you do." Tammie Dean cocked her head. "Now, isn't there someone else you need to keep informed? Someone who's taken care of you all your life?"

Holly's gaze widened. Her grandmother was up on all counts. "My father?"

"Why don't you invite him for Christmas, too? That way there will be another responsible adult here who is concerned about your well being, too."

"I'll call him right away." Holly glanced at the floor. "He may demand I come back home immediately. Just before I came here, there was a bomb at his house, and now I'm worried it was intended for me rather than for him."

"Wait one second, Missy. What's this about a bomb?"

Holly's gaze shot to Slade's. The mild panicked expression told her all she needed to know. "Slade didn't tell you."

It was a statement. Not a question.

Her grandmother replied, "I do not like being left in the dark. I may be an older woman, and I may have been in the hospital, but I deserve to be kept informed."

"I apologize. I had hoped to keep you from worrying."

Tammie Dean shot him an annoyed look. "So I'm worrying, and it would be easier on all of us if I was up to date on what I need to worry about."

"My dad is a retired district attorney."

"Believe me, honey, I know all that."

"Well, sometimes people he sent to jail are unhappy and decide they need revenge. So, the bomb ..."

"Was it a large bomb? Was anyone injured?"

"Everyone is okay. But, now I can't help wondering—"

"Both of us are wondering," cut in Slade.

"If I'm the target and not my dad. Someone has it in for me here, and maybe it started in Fort Worth."

"Have you done anything to make someone feel your death is a good solution to their problems?"

"No, ma'am. Maybe I should leave before it becomes dangerous for anyone else. I could go some-where no one knows me."

"And how will that keep *you* safe?"

"Maybe the person doing this won't know where to find me?"

"Or maybe the person targeting you will have his or her own way with no one else there to protect you," said Slade.

"I don't care what you've gotten yourself into, young lady, but there are at least the three of us, Slade, your father and me, who are determined to keep you safe."

Holly wasn't sure what to think. Perhaps her being near anyone she loved meant that they weren't safe, either.

"I can see those stubborn wheels in your head starting to turn, Holly," said Slade. "No. You need to stay where we can keep you safe. If you're worried about Tammie Dean, you can come back to my ranch where the security measures are already in place."

"If my dad comes for Christmas, then I'd like to remain here with him, if I may, Tammie Dean?"

"Of course, hon. Don't you worry. Just give him a call and tell him what's going on. I'm sure he'll want to join us."

It was going to take a whole lot of explaining to her dad. This was one phone call she dreaded.

CHAPTER SEVENTEEN

That evening Holly grabbed Lobo's lead and led him outside to do his business before bed. As they stepped off the back porch and onto a grassy strip behind the house, Holly chewed her lip.

She had been completely mistaken about the difficulty level of her phone call home. At first she'd invited him to come for Christmas Eve and Christmas, and he'd sounded very enthusiastic.

But. He'd nearly gone off his rocket when he heard about the cookies. Between that and the earlier fire, she feared he'd grab her through the telephone line.

She'd offered to go home, but he'd told her to stay put.

She'd offered to disappear somewhere no one would find her, and at that one, his anger was palpable.

He'd said, "If Tammie Dean will have me, I'm coming in the morning."

Holly was sure her grandmother would be pleased to have him, but Holly wasn't sure she wanted to deal with him. He'd probably follow her every footstep.

She'd explained that a basic security system had been installed, and cameras and monitors were going in the next day or two. The security personnel had been busy and underfoot most of the day, but that hadn't satisfied her dad.

She'd told him it was only a few days until they were expecting him, but he wouldn't be deterred. "I'll get a hotel room if necessary."

She'd given in then. "It won't be necessary. Tammie Dean will be happy to have you. Just don't arrive too early. It's too late tonight to talk with Tammie Dean about you coming, and we'll need to get a room ready."

"I'll call before I leave the house."

"Thanks, Dad. I love you."

"I love you, too. Now get some sleep."

After they hung up, Holly had mixed feelings. She was secretly relieved her dad was coming, but she didn't want him thinking she needed more protection. Her frustration had been there in the phone ether between them. She felt rather guilty over it, but she didn't need another keeper. Between Tammie Dean, Slade, Millie and even Lobo, she was more than well looked after.

At that moment Lobo stopped what he was doing and emitted a low-pitched growl. He began barking toward the trees and a small clearing in the field to the left of the strip of grass. With each bark, his little body seemed to hop, almost as if he were bobbing in the grass.

"What is it, Lobo?" Holly asked, looking where the dog was indicating, but it was too dark for her to see anything. Maybe it was a deer or some other type of wildlife? From all the life-sized posters in the area, it could even be Bigfoot. Although it more resembled the size of a human—or a bear.

Either way, the barking made her nervous. Lobo should be done with his business, so Holly called him to come in. "Come on, Lobo. Let's go."

Lobo ran up to Holly, but turned around and delivered a final volley of barks before he went through the door Holly held open, and back into the house.

The little dog ran ahead of her to the stairs, but Holly held back after locking the back door and setting the security alarm. She glanced through the sheer curtains, but still didn't see anything.

Lobo's reaction had been strange.

Holly shivered, then headed up to bed, feeling grateful both that Slade was staying with them and that the security had been installed.

As she glanced down the hall, she saw Slade had poked his head out of his bedroom door. "Everything good?"

"Yes. Good night and sweet dreams," she called back to him, relaxed in the face of so much concern.

"Sleep well," he called back in a low-voiced rumble that sent lovely rumbles down her spine.

The next morning when Holly headed downstairs with Lobo, she very specifically wanted to make sure it was okay with her grandmother if her father came today.

Tammie Dean wasn't likely to refuse, but Holly wanted to make sure it truly was fine with her.

After a quick visit to the grassy strip for Lobo to do his business, Holly was pleased to see that the pup wasn't disturbed this morning, nor did he bark at anything. Holly herself didn't have that awful feeling of being watched, either. Lobo seemed full of himself, dashing after leaves blowing in the wind and pounding his little paws as if he was drawing a line in the leaves.

Once they returned inside, Holly expected to see Tammie Dean when she entered the kitchen, but only Millie was there.

"Good morning," she greeted her, her elbows up to the edges of a bowl she was mixing something in.

"Morning," said Holly in response. "Where are Slade and Tammie Dean? I thought they'd be here."

"You beat Tammie Dean, but Slade's out working already. Those security people are with him, and Slade's suggesting where the cameras should be installed."

"That's good." When she saw Slade, she'd tell him about the grass strip behind the house and see if he was installing a camera there or not.

"How about some French Toast for breakfast?"

Holly's mouth watered. "That sounds delicious."

As Millie busied around the stove, Tammie Dean entered the kitchen wreathed in smiles. "Good morning glory!"

Holly grinned. She loved that old saying. "It *is* a good morning."

"There's a whole lot of banging going on out front. Looks like the security company is busy."

"Yes, Ms. Nelson. Slade's out with them."

Tammie Dean batted at Millie with her napkin. "I don't know who gave you permission to call me *Ms. Nelson* like some fancy hooptidoo person, Millie, but to you I'm *Tammie Dean*, just like I am to everyone in the family."

"All right already, Tammie Dean, although that's going to be hard to remember since I've been calling you Ms. Nelson all my life."

"Not to my face, you haven't."

"No, ma'am."

"I have something I need to talk with you about, Tammie Dean," Holly said quietly. It was time to let her know about her dad.

Her grandmother reached out and tapped Holly on the arm. "What's on your mind, hon?"

"As you instructed, I called my dad last night."

"Good job."

"He said to thank you for the invitation for Christmas Eve and Christmas. He's honored to be included with the family."

"That's sweet of him, but I expected nothing less

from the man who did such a wonderful job raising my granddaughter."

"You both ready for your French Toast?" asked Millie.

Holly picked up her napkin and placed it in her lap as Millie served them. The aroma was incredible. "About my dad—"

"Go on, child." Tammie Dean slathered her toast with butter.

"He was—upset when I told him about the recent events here." Holly didn't want to say too much because she wasn't certain Millie was fully aware of what had been happening.

"I'm not at all surprised."

"He wants to come sooner. Today, actually."

"You call that man immediately and reassure him that he is most welcome to come whenever he wants. If I were in his shoes, I'd want to make sure my child was being properly looked after. Get out your phone and call him right now."

"Let me finish my yummy French toast, and I'll call him right away."

After they ate breakfast, it didn't take long to reassure her dad that he could come and he was welcome. Tammie Dean instructed Holly about what she needed to do to get the room next door to hers ready, and where she could find the spare linens.

It took less than thirty minutes to prepare the bedroom for her dad. The room boasted a queen-sized bed, a dresser and two end tables, as well as an adjoining bathroom. Her dad would be totally comfortable, and now that Tammie Dean approved of his coming, Holly felt a lot better about the situation. She had missed her dad, and it would be comforting to have him nearby, especially if someone was targeting her.

By the time she returned downstairs, Slade had returned.

"Do you have all the cameras situated?" she asked.

"Mostly. There are a couple of areas where we may need to bring in an electrician, but I checked, then told him one of my cousins can do any wiring needed this afternoon.

"That's good. I wanted to mention that when I took Lobo out to do his business last night, he growled and barked at something or someone in the field to the left of the backdoor."

"Did you see what or who it was?"

"No, it was too dark. But it worried me. Do you think it could have been a bear?"

He shook his head. "Not a bear. Maybe a wildcat, or even a armadillo."

"It looked bigger. It could have been human." She wondered. Somehow the silhouette reminded her of the man who'd spied on her before. The area had been too shadowy to see anything for sure, but she'd certainly gotten the impression of something sizable. Since she couldn't make anything out, though, she couldn't say for sure that it was a man.

Her silence seemed to worry Slade. "Why don't I ask the security crew to point a camera in that direction? It won't be a big deal since they're already installing a couple of cameras on the back of the house anyway."

Holly smiled. "Good idea. Thank you."

CHAPTER EIGHTEEN

Seeing his granddaughter from a distance couldn't be more annoying. That child belonged to him. Right now she should be at his house, making his dinner or serving him a cold beer.

The fact his property touched the Nelson property made it a mite easier for him to keep his eye on things. Even though Tammie Dean had told him his granddaughter hadn't lived, he knew better now and going forward he'd keep in mind that no woman could be trusted, no matter how highfalutin she was.

He couldn't help but feel grateful that someone had tipped him off. The note told him to visit the graveyard and check on his granddaughter's plot. That had exposed the trickery in a way words could never do.

He seriously did not like being lied to in the best of times, and for the way Tammie Dean and her husband had treated him back then, he was far more than annoyed. He was snake-eyed pissed.

He knew how to get even though.

His granddaughter should not be living high on the hog like she was at Tammie Dean's. And the sooner the girl learned her proper place in life—taking care of her granddaddy—the better off she would be. The girl was just as uppity as Wendy, but he'd taught her mama. And he'd learn Holly. Why, even her name showed how uppity she was.

He smiled. Her nose wouldn't be sticking up in the air for long.

Not if his name was Farraday.

Holly couldn't help the wide grin on her face when she greeted her dad late that afternoon.

When he grabbed her in a hug, Holly was relieved that he didn't look at all tired from the long drive from Fort Worth.

He said, "You're a sight for sore eyes, pet."

"You are, too," she replied, stepping back and drinking in his sweet face. She took his arm. "Come on in and meet Tammie Dean."

"I'm looking forward to meeting the woman who made it possible for me to have a daughter like you."

"You charmer. I bet you say that to all the girls."

As Holly led him through the house to the family

room where Tammie Dean was sitting with her feet up, Holly was filled with excitement. This was joining the two sectors of her life together in a way that was both thrilling and worrisome. What if her dad and her grandmother didn't like each other?

They stepped into the room, and, by the expression on Tammie Dean's face, Holly realized she had nothing to worry about. Tammie Dean's smile indicated her approval of, and maybe a little bit of a crush on, Holly's dad.

"Dad, I'd like you to meet my grandmother, Tammie Dean Nelson." They all made short work of the introductions and rather than handshaking, lots of hugs were spread around.

Her dad had only arrived a few days before the other guests, but Holly was exceedingly grateful that her grandmother was more than willing to welcome him. It made her a little sad that she hadn't grown up knowing Tammie Dean, but what she knew of her now, she adored.

Later that afternoon, Slade arrived at the house and Holly couldn't help but light up a little at the sight of him. What was it about him that made her like him so much?

He offered his hand to her dad. "Nice to see you Mr. Brown."

"Call me Al, please. Everyone does."

"Very well, sir—Al."

"I hear you've been trying to look after my girl, and while it's been successful, it hasn't always been easy."

"I've done my best, but have to admit *I* haven't always been as successful as I would like. Why don't we step into the office where I can go into more detail."

"Why do I feel like the two of you are going to talk about me behind my back?"

"I'm planning to show him the security measures we've taken, Holly, and if you want to come, you're welcome."

CHAPTER NINETEEN

Relief trickled down Slade's spine as he led Holly's father outside. For once he had positive progress to report.

Up until now he felt like a complete failure. He'd promised to look after Holly, and she'd been subjected to a fire and poison-laced cookies. There was no telling what else he may have missed.

But now, at the ranch, safety precautions were in place.

Mr. Brown nodded. "You've done a great job with the security cameras."

"Thank you, sir. I'm doing my best to take better care of your daughter."

Mr. Brown clapped him on the back. "I know you have, son. Holly couldn't have been in more careful hands. But now I'm here, and between the two of us, she'll have double the protection."

"Yes, sir."

"So, is that a camera over there?"

"It's where we're adding one, but it hasn't been installed yet."

Meanwhile, Holly and Tammie Dean watched the two men through the back windows.

Each of them pointed at various points in the area surrounding the house, and at times each of them waved his arms while speaking. It was almost as if they were pantomiming each other.

"It looks like they're getting along."

"You bet," said Tammie Dean. "They are united in their efforts to look after you. They'll be best friends by this afternoon. You'll see."

Holly grinned as the two men fist bumped. "I suspect you're right."

"Are you ready to go up to the attic and dig out the stockings?"

"Do we get to hang them on the chimney with care?"

Tammie Dean gave her a mischievous grin. "Oh, even better."

"Yeah?" asked Holly.

Tammie Dean dimpled. "You'll see. Follow me."

Within minutes they'd climbed a couple of stair-cases to reach a doorway to the attic. As they stepped in, Holly was surprised to see how spacious the room was, and how much light filtered in through several Cape Cod style windows. "What a nice room. Almost too nice to be referred to as an attic."

While there was a fair amount of unused furniture in the space, she also glimpsed a whole lot of wheeled suitcases as well as wheeled plastic bins. If there was any dust in the attic, it was sparse.

"I suppose it could be used for other things than as an attic, and there was talk, between me and Conrad, of using it as a schoolroom if we ever needed to home-school our kids. Who would have thought how life changes in an almost complete circle ..."

"Good point." Tammie Dean seemed to be very philosophical that morning, but Holly had no plan to mention it. This sort of introspection was likely usual in cases of those who had survived life-threatening illness or were facing it. If Tammie Dean wanted to talk about it, Holly was more than available with an ear, but until then, she wouldn't drag her grandmother into such deep discussions. "Now, where do we find the stockings? I didn't see anything that could be them near where we got the tree decorations or the outdoor lights."

Tammie Dean indicated a large wheeled suitcase beneath the center window cut out. "That's it, over there."

Holly didn't say it, but couldn't help but boggle over the idea that Christmas stockings had been packed in a very large suitcase—and it appeared to be a designer one at that given the insignia and logos printed all over it. She approached the bag and raised the handle. "This one?"

"You bet. What do you think of their storage container?" She giggled.

"This suitcase?"

"Ye-es."

"I think it's a super nice container. Are the stockings valuable?"

Tammie Dean tilted her head toward her right shoulder. "To me they are extremely valuable. They go back to my mother's time."

The two women left the attic and began descending the stairs to the ground floor. At last reaching it, Tammie Dean indicated that Holly should follow her into the formal living room. At the far end of it was a huge fireplace, large enough for several grown men to stand together inside of it.

"Wow. Just wow."

Tammie Dean leaned over and began to unzip the suitcase. Had Holly mentioned it was a very large suitcase? And apparently it was filled with dozens of Christmas stockings, each one of which carefully had a name inscribed. "You remember the people you called? Everyone has a stocking."

"Wow. I'm stunned."

Tammie Dean reached behind the sofa and pulled out a bag. "Everyone has a stocking. Even you."

She handed Holly the bag. "Look inside."

Holly slowly peeked into the bag and couldn't believe her eyes. Within seconds she held the most beautiful Christmas stocking she had ever seen. And her name was inscribed on it in a multicolored fabric. There was white fur at the top, and the bottom was made up of layers of silk and tulle and satin and ornamented with both glittery rhinestones and pearls. It was drop dead gorgeous.

A tear rolled down her cheek. "I appreciate the gift so much, Tammie Dean. How can I thank you?"

"You already have." Tammie Dean brushed back tears. "I'm relieved you like your stocking. I ordered it before we met and I wasn't sure it would be to your taste."

"It's exactly my taste."

"We're so much alike." Tammie Dean patted Holly's shoulder. "I'd know you were my kin even if I didn't know how we were related."

"I was thinking exactly that myself. When I studied the photograph of the family at the guest house, which by the way wasn't harmed, thankfully, I wondered if I would have a sense of knowing you, and other family members, regardless of the knowledge we are related." She gave Tammie Dean a little squeeze. "I think I would."

"So, where would you like to hang your stocking? It goes up first." Tammie Dean indicated the little hooks that had been hung beneath the huge fireplace mantle so that they barely showed. It was a great idea for hanging stockings without having to make new nail holes each year. But there were sure a lot of them. There needed to be considering the number of stockings in the suitcase she'd lugged down from the attic.

"Do you want your stocking in the middle?"

"No way. How about yours goes in the middle. Considering how everyone is so thankful you're back home from the hospital in time to celebrate Christmas, it's only fitting."

"Alrighty. So maybe Bridget can be on my left side, and you on my right. Then I'll divide them up into family units and you'll know what to hang next."

That seemed okay to Holly, so she got busy. Forty-five minutes later, they appeared to be done. "There. Is each stocking in the right order?"

"It's perfect." Tammie Dean grinned ear to ear. "Thank you so much for your help. There is no way I could have gotten everything done without your help."

"I'm only too happy to do whatever you need. We all want you to get well and back to full strength again."

"Here, here," came a male voice.

Holly turned to see who spoke, and it was Tammie Dean's son-in-law, Jameson Wilson, Bridget's husband. She supposed that technically he was her uncle by marriage. But calling him by the moniker didn't feel comfortable.

Tammie Dean said, "Hello, Jameson. How are you?"

"I'm doing great as long as your health is improving."

"Hello, Jameson," added Holly. She reminded herself that he's a family member and she needed to be polite. Also, his sons had been very helpful to her during and after the fire. Being courteous was the very least she could do. "You look well."

"Call me Uncle." Jameson showed his teeth. It wasn't really a smile. More like a painful grimace. "Thank you. I've been getting in my daily workouts at the gym."

"Good for you."

"Did you need me for something?" asked Tammie Dean.

He wagged a handful of documents at her. "I just have a couple of things for your signature. But if you're busy, I could wait, or you could just sign them?"

Tammie Dean gave him *the look*. The kind of look that says *don't talk nonsense*. "We're about done here, Holly. I'll catch up with you later, okay?"

"No problem. I need to take Lobo to do his business anyway." She turned and left the living room with the dog who had been sleeping on a cushion nearby. "Come on, Lobo. Let's go outside."

CHAPTER TWENTY

Farraday watched Slade and Mr. Brown, Holly's supposed father, but he knew Brown wasn't her real father.

Pulling the blue Post-It from his pocket, he scanned the notes written there, then nodded. Holly belonged to him, just like her mama had, and her mama before her.

Lying Nelsons couldn't change the fact she was *his* granddaughter. The note said so. Now what was it that his friend had suggested? Oh, yeah. The dog. The way to the girl was through the dog.

He fingered the tennis ball in his pocket. He didn't know of any dog who could resist a ball like this one. Wendy's dog. No, that wasn't right. Her daughter's dog. Holly. That was right. Holly's dog wouldn't be able to resist since it was a small tennis ball, just right for the sissy mongrel.

He nodded and walked closer to the Nelson property.

That had been strange. Holly opened the backdoor to let herself and Lobo back inside. It wasn't like Lobo to disobey, but there had been a couple of moments when she thought Lobo was going to run away toward the back of the property.

Holly glanced at the cameras mounted near the back door. They were a relief. As she entered the house, Slade called out to her.

"Howdy."

"Hey." Holly and Lobo entered the house, and Lobo ran off toward the kitchen. He was probably in search of a treat. They'd been plentiful while Christmas dishes were being prepared.

Slade tilted his head toward the front of the house. "I think I just saw your handiwork."

"What do you mean?"

"The stockings."

"Oh, yeah. I helped Tammie Dean with them." They walked together to the living room. "Did I do them justice?"

"You did better than I ever did. Tammie Dean always refused to allow me to help because apparently I'm a disaster at correct stocking placement."

Holly giggled and took a seat in front of the fireplace, which now crackled with newly laid and lit firewood. "I'm certain that's not true."

Slade tapped her shoulder with his as he took a seat beside her.

Outside the room, Al Brown watched as his daughter flirted with Slade Colfax. He wasn't sure whether to feel thrilled or threatened by how much his daughter apparently liked the man. As far as other men go, Slade appeared to be one of the good ones. But if he ever gave Holly cause to regret—

"Look how cute they are," whispered Tammie Dean in his ear.

"So that's how it is." Al grimaced down at Holly's grandmother. He couldn't work up any enthusiasm, though. "Cute."

Tammie Dean nodded, a dreamy expression on her face. "I wish I had thought of it, because I couldn't have done better had I actually planned it."

"So you approve?"

"Is there any reason why I shouldn't approve of my own granddaughter?" she snapped back at him.

"That wasn't what I meant."

She stared at him as if shocked. "Surely you don't dislike my sweet Slade?"

"You're certain he's a good man?"

"He's the best. Like I said, I couldn't have done better if I had planned this myself."

CHAPTER TWENTY-ONE

Farraday thumped his chest with pleasure at the steps he'd taken and the praise he'd been given for all his attempts to bring Holly home. Although the steps had for the most part failed, he'd made valiant attempts to complete them. And not everything had failed. He had big plans in the works.

Patting his pocket, he reminded himself of the sticky note located there. He'd been encouraged to keep up his efforts despite the latest security measures. He had every legal right to stand on his own property—and if he saw Holly or Lobo again, he wouldn't cross over the boundary. He'd call them to him.

All women were alike, so it wouldn't be difficult. All he had to say was that he had something important to show her. That would get her attention. She'd join him out of camera range in mere minutes. Then it wouldn't take any time at all for him to lock her or the dog or both into an outbuilding.

No one would hear either of them there, then he could use his persuaders—left and right fists—to teach them everything they needed to know about obedience. And he figured they didn't currently know much.

As long as Holly didn't piss him off too much, like her Mama had taken great pains to do, Holly wouldn't lose her good looks or teeth.

It was child's play really.

The note he'd found on his breakfast table yesterday morning said to make his move on Christmas Eve after the party began. The family would be too busy to notice Holly's absence.

Farraday smiled and thumped his chest again.

CHAPTER TWENTY-TWO

Holly did a walkthrough of the house, going from room to bedroom to baths, checking to see that each was ready for family to arrive.

The following day was Christmas Eve, and she didn't want to be frantically getting everything ready.

The beds had been made, the guestrooms even had small holiday decorations to make them even cozier.

For some reason, maybe it was because of the obvious affection from Tammie Dean, this Christmas was more important to Holly than any she'd experienced as an adult. Having her Dad here made the experience even better.

The next morning, the aroma of freshly baking sugar cookies filled the air, along with visions of sugarplums dancing in Holly's head. There was no season better than Christmas, and the celebration of Jesus's birth, and the best of all was Christmas Eve, when anything feels possible—such as Peace on Earth. From the more worldly side, gifts, sweets, delicious food, family gatherings were in great demand. It truly was the best of all times of the year.

People began arriving that morning, not only at the Nelson Ranch, but also at Slade's ranch since the guesthouse was out of commission this year due to the fire damage. However, between the main ranch house and all of the bunkhouses, there remained plenty of room for the extended family members to stay comfortably.

Slade side-stepped and ducked his head as he entered Tammie Dean's kitchen, in order to avoid the big ball of mistletoe which had been provided by, he assumed, his cousin Maria, who was a huge romantic and, at times, an even bigger practical joker. No telling what she had planned. She stood in the far corner of the kitchen, pointing at the ball, and he asked her, "Hope springs eternal?"

"You betcha. Whatever it takes. I've tried online dating without success. So if I have to move onto parasitical plants, I've got it covered."

He shook his head at her. One of these days some guy would be lucky enough to claim her hand. Slade and her other cousins would do their best to make sure the claimant was deserving. "Whatever works."

"You think I'm silly enough to trust some herb to supply my happiness?"

"It wasn't you?"

"Nope," said Maria. "It was Holly."

"Oh, yeah?" His heart skipped a beat.

He watched as a sly smile crossed Maria's face. "So is there something going on that I need to know about in those quarters?"

He and Maria were pretty close, having spent much of their childhood under the same roof. He valued her opinion and didn't know how to answer at first, then he nodded. "I sure hope there could be."

She beamed at him. "Smart man."

CHAPTER TWENTY-THREE

Holly had hit it off with Charlie Nelson Murphy during their phone conversation. As a teacher, Holly had a lot in common with new mothers. And, as cousins, their interests mostly aligned.

Holly had explained that she was Charlie's cousin, Harlan Nelson's only child. Then she'd had to explain (to everyone she called), that she was adopted and not dead and buried.

Charlie told Holly all about birthing her first child. Little Davis Jr. was just shy of nine months old. The upcoming Christmas would be his first, and Charlie was incredibly excited about it.

Davis Jr. had already pulled himself upright and it was only a matter of *when* he began to walk. It could be any day.

Holly grinned. Holidays were so much nicer when small children were involved.

Once Charlie arrived at the Nelson Ranch, she gave Holly a tremendous hug while her husband held the baby and watched them with a bemused expression. Davis personified a new and doting dad.

Holly returned Charlie's hug, knowing she'd just made a new and long-lasting friendship. Before she could let go and step back, someone rudely yanked her away from Charlie.

Aunt Bridgette!

The older woman directed herself to Charlie. "I see you've met—Harlan's daughter."

"You bet. I'm so excited to have such a fantastic and likeable cousin in our family."

"If you say so," Aunt Bridgette replied, with a look-ing-down-her-nose gaze at Holly. "Now, you and Davis —and is this darling baby also Davis?—head on into the kitchen. Tammie Dean is holding court there, and she's going to absolutely adore your new little one."

As Charlie and her family followed Aunt Bridgette's bidding, the older woman had the temerity to turn back and smirk at Holly.

Holly had already received much more than a mere impression that Aunt Bridgette 1) didn't like Holly and 2) resented her. But now for the first time, Holly wondered if her aunt had been behind on the attempts on Holly's life. Although how she'd come up with the formula for a bomb, Holly had no idea. Maybe there was something lying around at her homestead?

It would pay to keep an eye on Bridgette and remain extra vigilant whenever her aunt was nearby.

Holly's life could depend up on it.

Especially since Aunt Bridgette had insisted on locking Lobo up in Holly's bedroom...

Slade brushed aside a feeling of foreboding. He wasn't sure exactly why. Perhaps it was the prior attempts on Holly's life. Or the fact that nothing untoward had happened during the last week. Perhaps the additional security arrangements had made a difference.

But his past experience didn't foreshadow the ill-wishers just going away. Not after everything he or she had already done. Nothing had occurred that pointed to one sex or another, although poisoning generally was a woman's favored method of murder.

Monty Joe joined him in holding up the wall behind them. They gave each other fist bumps.

"Happy Christmas," Monty Joe said.

"Same to you." He eyed the man. "You're looking happy and well fed. Marriage suits you."

"Yep. Lori has brought a lot of laughter and joy my way. Plus I acquired another 300 acres—my Christmas present to myself. So I'm definitely feeling the holiday spirit."

Monty Joe eyed Slade. "Now you, big guy, aren't looking so hot."

Slade curled his lip. He hadn't realized his discontent was so visible. "I'm worrying."

"You don't usually look like this—as if a rattler had you in his sights."

"We've installed oodles of cameras, motion sensors and so on, yet I can't get the feeling of dread to go away. I can't shake it."

"I'd stake my new 300 acres on your instincts, Slade. If you think so, then there is definitely something to worry about."

"Well, it's time for our white elephant exchange Christmas to start. Maybe afterwards I can get your help."

"You got it."

The family white elephant Christmas exchange was a custom of *legend*.

On Christmas morning, the family would unwrap Santa's gifts. But on Christmas Eve, it was all about the naughtiness.

Every year each person brought a gift with a value under $20. You wanted to bring something that people would seriously want. Everyone drew a number from Conrad Nelson's old cowboy hat. Each number was called out by Tammy Dean. When it was their turn, they would choose a gift, unwrap it, and then decide whether to keep it or exchange it from a previously wrapped gift.

The family had been doing this since before Slade

was born, and family members were known to collude and connive to get the gift of their desire. Particularly popular were gifts involving alcohol, food or candy, but most have evolved into gift bags rather than a singular item, and lots of folks crafted their own holiday designs.

CHAPTER TWENTY-FOUR

As Bobby Gray and Deputy Max Wilson (Aunt Bridgette's son) fought over a full-length apron depicting a topless He-Man, Holly decided it was past time to get Lobo and take him out to do his business.

She quickly snuck out and headed to her bedroom. Lobo greeted her with a series of bounces and little squeaky barks highlighting each bounce.

"Are you ready to do your business, little one?"

Another yip told her everything she needed to know.

Gathering him, his leash and a small ball, she headed down the backstairs, then out the backdoor.

The house was incredibly noisy and she was grateful to get a break from all of the racket. They were happy cries and hollers, and music, but a little much for her. She'd grown up as an only child. Holidays were just as quiet as the rest of the year in a one-child household.

Stepping outdoors, she was startled to see it had been silently snowing. At least an inch already covered the ground and branches. While it wasn't unheard of in west Texas, certainly a White Christmas wasn't the norm and hadn't been expected, at least as far as she was aware.

The snowflakes were large and wet, and dusted Lobo's fur and Holly's hair and lashes. How beautiful the dark night was.

Lobo dashed ahead, yapping at the snow, then carefully doing his business as if he were afraid his little paws would get wet.

What was that noise? Holly wasn't sure whether the sound had come from the distance, in which Lobo was now running at full pace, or from inside the house—the decibel level coming from inside was off the chart.

"Lobo," she called and stepped toward the rear of the property where Lobo stood his ground and began yap-bouncing again.

Just then, her Dad came outside and joined her. "How you holding up, kiddo?"

"I'm fine. Just enjoying a few minutes of peace. Plus it's gorgeous out here. A White Christmas!"

"It's pretty remarkable." His breath came out in a fog from the cold night. "Are you just about done out here? They were two numbers from yours when I stepped out here."

"You bet, Dad."

She called Lobo and at first he hesitated. On her

second command, he turned around and rushed back to her side. It took awhile because he'd covered a lot of distance, more than she'd realized. Regret over what she needed to do filled her. "Sorry, pup. It's back in my bedroom for you."

"That seems harsh," said her dad.

"Aunt Bridgette insisted—and you know, with the place so noisy and crowded, it's probably the wisest course."

He nodded and opened the back door for them.

It was as if a bullhorn sounded, the cacophony was more than deafening—it was 777-level blast.

"It's almost your turn to choose a gift. I'll take Lobo up to your room so you can join the tumult."

"Thanks, Dad. I don't want to miss my chance at the exchange."

"Got your eye on something?"

"You bet. I loved the Old English village cottage. Too cute."

Bridgette look up and narrowed her eyes as Holly rejoined the family. She'd hoped to lose the interloper, but no such luck.

She'd done everything possible to discourage the young woman, who, for all intents and purposes, was born on the wrong side of the blanket. Certainly, she was conceived there.

She shot her husband *the look*.

The look that spoke volumes and conveyed the message that it was time to make whatever move was necessary to rid the family of the nuisance.

Jameson gave her a slow nod and the smile he sent her sent shivers up and down her own spine.

She only hoped Farraday had been convinced to come collect his grandchild. The sooner the better.

From the adoring look on Tammie Dean's face, Holly's departure couldn't come too soon.

Cousin Bobby Gray had taken over the calling from Tammie Dean. "Number sweet sixteen!"

"That's my number," cried Holly, bouncing from her seat on the sofa.

"Go find yourself a present, Holly," exclaimed Charlie. Now cousin Charlie was a shining example of exemplary young womanhood, unlike Holly. The fake probably wasn't even a schoolteacher as she claimed.

Holly made a move to trade a wrapped gift for the village cottage from Aunt Bridgette, but Slade stopped her. "You need to unwrap the gift first." Then in a whisper he added, "Besides you never want to take anything from Aunt Bridgette. Otherwise, you'll hear about it for the rest of your life—and it wouldn't be fun or pretty."

CHAPTER TWENTY-FIVE

Farraday banged his fist on the nearest fence post. How could he have missed snaring the little yappy dog? It should have been fool's play—and he'd failed. Obviously it was Holly's fault—no, no, he corrected himself. Obviously it was Wendy's fault. He'd add it to the list of her sins that required reparations. Wendy was being far too highfalutin since rubbing elbows with the Nelsons. He wasn't having it. His daughter would best remember who ruled the roost in his household.

Teaching her the error of her ways would be entertaining. It always had been. His spirit soared. He'd educate her soon. Very soon, now.

He stood in the kitchen doorway. Pondering.

Only one question remained. **Could Farraday be trusted to finish off the girl?**

The answer was **No**.

But there was plenty of time to act.

Plenty.

He nodded his head and returned to the living room. The time to act would arrive shortly. He grinned, relieved it would soon come to an end.

Slade had to bite back his laughter when Holly put back the unwrapped gift she'd been holding and selected another. As she opened it, it was soon revealed to be another Old English cottage, but this one had to have violated the gifting maximum because it was part of a collector's edition.

Holly hugged it to her chest, then rocked it like a baby. "I love it," she squealed at Charlie Nelson Davis. "I love, love it."

Charlie cradled her newborn, who didn't seem to mind the noise level at all. He gurgled, beaming a drooly grin and clapped his hands while staring at Holly. The baby was such a cutie, and he was really smart. Slade wished he could get away with staring at Holly in the same way.

Davis sat next to them, but he paid no attention to anyone other than Charlie and the babe. His gaze was filled with adoration.

Man, he had it bad.

But, wondered Slade as he wiped a matching adoring gaze off his face, did Slade have it just as bad for Holly?

He'd originally pegged her as a city girl, and while she was raised in Fort Worth, nothing about her behavior had seemed the least bit snooty. In fact, she appeared to love everything about the Nelson Ranch and its members.

Did he have it bad for Holly?

He grimaced. So what if he did? The woman reminded him of rays of sunshine glowing into the dark corners of his soul. He had every reason to adore her.

CHAPTER TWENTY-SIX

By the time the gift exchange was completed, the din and racket began to tone down a little—but only a little. Holly fought off a headache, then decided some fresh air would likely help.

Who knew that having a dog could be so useful in terms of an excuse. Slade caught her eye as she made her way from the overcrowded room.

"Taking Lobo out?" he asked.

"It's more a case of taking myself out, but that's my excuse if anyone asks where I've gone. I'm definitely taking Lobo out." She grinned widely. "I don't want to disappoint Tammie Dean by slipping out too often."

"Don't worry. Take your time. If she starts asking for you I'll come out and let you know."

She patted his arm, and when she did so, the sparks between them flared, making her stumble slightly. They were so overdue for taking things to the next level, the next step. Like way overdue.

But for now, she truly needed some quiet time. As much as she was growing to adore her new family, she preferred them only a few at a time as opposed to a huge stable filled with them.

After grabbing Lobo from her bedroom, she rushed back downstairs. When she stepped out the back door she shivered.

Along with the snow, the temperature had also dropped. On the eastern sky, snow clouds still blocked the heavens. Lobo ran ahead into the yard, his little legs leaving doll-like tiny puppy dog prints in the snow.

The other half of the heavens was clearing and a large, bright moon shimmered in the black sky.

That was the thing about the country at night—it was black dark. Twinkling stars emerged from the darkness, lighting up the night sky in a way that could never be duplicated in the city.

At the squeak of a door opening, she looked back and saw Slade.

"Just coming to check on you. Are you okay?"

"Fantastic."

"The family can be a bit—overwhelming."

"Yeah, but also endearing and adorable. The mix works for me."

"Good. Tammie Dean would be devastated if you didn't like them."

"No worries here."

Lobo yipped in the distance and ran further, more outside the area highlighted by the security lights.

"I'm still enjoying myself. Mind if I catch up with you when Lobo is done out here? He's been cooped up so long."

"No problem."

"We shouldn't be much longer."

Again, Lobo barked happily as he scrambled around in the field.

Slade smiled and ducked back inside as Holly spun to see what Lobo was up to now. He was abruptly quiet—totally not like him.

Trotting toward where she'd last seen Lobo, she called to him and whistled. No response.

Once, she thought she might have heard him scrambling in a bush, but it turned out to be a feral animal, like a raccoon, opossum or an armadillo.

She stepped closer, then saw up ahead that the snow had been disturbed. The footsteps and impressions in the snow weren't only those of Lobo. Human steps were mixed in and bits of snow was churned up, as if there'd been a scuffle.

She didn't hear a sound. Out of the blue, hair raised on the back of her neck. Danger. Somehow there was danger. She'd been through enough in her life to know to trust her instincts.

Rather than go forward, she turned and walked—quickly—back toward the ranch house and the brilliant beams of light shown from the security lights. They were a ways off, and she hightailed it.

As soon as she got back, she'd seek Slade and together they could find the dog. But being out here alone tonight, did not feel safe. Her heart pounded. What had set all of her senses into overdrive?

As she rounded a bend, Farraday stepped out from behind a mesquite tree.

Holly came to an abrupt stand still.

"Git yerself over here, girl, or I will kill your dog," he said, pulling Lobo from behind his back where he'd apparently been hiding him.

"Lobo!" she yelled.

The tiny pup bristled and bit Farraday, who dropped him.

Lobo yelped on landing, but seemed okay as he scrambled off into the brush.

This was Holly's chance to flee, too.

Her heart nearly fought its way out of her chest as she ran all out toward the house. Her grandfather had strength and cussedness to help him. Her youth and speed was what she had going for her.

Then, just as the back door came into view, someone or something stepped between her and the house.

A dark silhouette.

She glanced back. Farraday, she couldn't think of him as her grandfather, followed closely behind her— wheezily, but still chasing her. Facing the silhouette between her and safety as she ran, she couldn't make out who it was. Probably a man.

A coyote howled in the distance, sending fresh waves of shivers through her body.

She continued to close the expanse between the silhouette and herself. "Slade?"

Her answer was a laugh. A low, male laugh. Definitely not Slade.

Her breath froze in the frigid night air. The silhouette began to approach her, while drawing a weapon from his pocket—a pistol.

It was still too distant to see the type of gun, although, it *was* long-barreled and pointed directly at her.

First she said quick prayer for deliverance and requested the help of her guarding angel, then the training she'd received after being kidnapped kicked in. Thankfully.

Rather than presenting an easy shooting target, she began zigging and zagging her way, unexpectedly this way and then that, even going backwards at times, as she very, very gradually made her way forward.

Maintaining space between the gun and her would give her the best odds.

The snow chose that moment to start falling again, heavily, with huge wet flakes, making it difficult for the man to get a good sight on her.

As she evaded him, she sent up another prayer, this time of gratitude for the protective snow. Her guardian angel was looking after her as she'd requested. Hopefully he would remain with her the rest of the way to safety.

Given there was a gun in front of her and another man behind, her best bet was to rush toward the front of the house rather than the back as they would expect.

Her erratic zigzags seemed to annoy the man in front as he began following her zigzags. She ran full out for a pine tree. It would give her some cover as she chose her next move.

Everything was quiet and still for a few seconds, and she wondered if now she was safe, at least temporarily. Then her gaze picked up her own footsteps in the snow.

She had to move, fast, before the gun fired. The man realistically only had one shot because of the noise. Unless...

The gun fired in her direction and she saw the flash but heard only a dull thud. As she'd feared, unless—he had a silencer. And he did.

Her survival chances became more and more remote. No one would hear and know she was in trouble. However, the gun wasn't the only noisemaker.

She sprinted toward the front door and screamed as loudly as she was capable. "Help!

A door banged open as she zigzagged her way forward. "Help!"

The gun fired once more and missed her only by inches, sending splinters flying from a nearby mesquite tree.

Run directed her subconscience.

Screaming once more, she ran like her life depended on it, because it did. "Someone, please help!"

Another door banged and men's voices were audible over the pounding of her heart.

She made it to the front door of the ranch and didn't see where the voices were coming from, but the sounded nearby.

She dashed inside, locking the door behind her.

Then she heard Slade's voice, "Mr. Wilson?"

Another male voice said, "Dad?"

Another voice said, "There's Farraday, too."

Could Uncle Jameson be her assailant? As the voices grew louder, she heard him saying he'd come to assist her. Next, she heard Slade ask, "With a drawn gun?"

Taking a deep breath, she stepped back outdoors. Time to confront her uncle and Farraday.

EPILOGUE

Slade and the others immediately removed the pistol from Uncle Jameson's possession. He fought both Slade and his sons, trying to evade capture, but they prevailed.

As details emerged, it became evident that Uncle Jameson had been siphoning off money from the Nelson estate. Tammie Dean had been too trusting to delve into the ranch books, accepting her son-in-law at face value.

With her illness, and in time her eventual death, he was safe from audit once his wife inherited. The will directed that the ranch and assets would go to the oldest line's oldest heir—a ranked order of succession passing like a royal title—to the eldest child or if he were deceased, to his children.

Holly's existance totally messed up his plans. The estate would eventually go only to her as the heir from the eldest line, thus triggering a financial audit during probate.

He hadn't hidden his tracks, safe in the thought he'd never have to account for his false monetary dealings.

Holly sat huddled on a big living room sofa, covered in a soft blanket that Slade had tucked her into. He'd done the same for Tammie Dean, settled across the room on the opposite sofa.

The huge clock over the fireplace mantel (and the stockings stuffed and ready for morning, Christmas morning) indicated it was after four o'clock a.m.

Within a few hours, everyone would return to the Nelson Ranch for breakfast and opening gifts and stockings. Now, however, it was too late or perhaps, depending on how you thought about it, too early to crawl upstairs to get some sorely needed sleep.

"Why don't you get a nap, hon?" asked her Dad who came into the living room from the kitchen, apparently with the same idea.

"I'm good." And she was. Although tired, she was far too wired to get any rest at all. Why don't you head upstairs and grab one?"

"I think I will," he replied. "Consider grabbing some shut-eye, too." He squeezed her knee through the thick blanket, then made for the stairs.

Holly scooched deeper into the sofa. Maybe she should go to her bedroom. At least she could take a shower, but honestly, with the adrenaline continuing to flow through her veins, sleep was out of the question.

Just then Slade joined her. Tammie Dean snored quietly from her couch and Slade made a shushing motion with a finger over his lips, drawing her gaze to his mouth. He looked so welcoming and warm, as if one embrace from him would comfort her shivering body.

He gave her a slow smile and whispered, "Come with me?"

She nodded and rose, draping the blanket around her shoulders. He led her into the empty kitchen.

Pulling her into his arms, he situated them beneath a large clump of mistletoe dangling from above, then wordlessly closed the distance between them.

His lips gentled hers in the softest of caresses. Good heavens. A little kiss could do this? She thought she might float right up to heaven and beyond. Maybe her guardian angel was still on duty. It certainly felt that way to her, like she could melt into a puddle at Slade's feet.

He deepened the kiss, then gradually backed away from her, although she remained in the bow of his arms. "Merry Christmas, Holly. Something tells me this is just the first of a lifetime of Christmases we will spend together."

"You think?"

"Don't you?"

Tammie Dean soundlessly came up behind them, arm in arm with Holly's dad. "We all think."

"We worried that the happenings tonight would put you off. I'm thrilled Slade is going to persuade you otherwise."

Holly gazed into his eyes. "You think?"

"Definitely." Then he kissed her, right there in front of her dad and grandmother, as if he'd never let her go. And she knew she never would. She knew her mother and father had to be smiling down on them from above.

Just then they heard the sound of bells.

Lobo came dashing into the kitchen, covered in holly, red ribbon and bells.

Slade laughed. "Either an angel earned his wings—or the ring camera just got tripped."

Holly grinned broadly, so happy to be alive and surrounded by those she loved. It was the perfect beginning to a soon to be perfect lifetime. "Merry Christmas!"

THE END

Ho, Ho, Ho! Merry Christmas!

For me, writing fun books is like eating ice cream. They're delicious, fun and go down easy. I love getting to spend time with the quirky characters who populate my stories. I hope you get as much of a kick out of them as I do writing them.

Please help other readers discover my books by recommending the series to friends or family members who you think will enjoy them, too. Another way to help spread the word is by writing a review and letting other readers know what you liked about the story. Please consider leaving a review for *Christmas at Nelson Ranch*. I'd very much appreciate it!

Happy Reading and Merry Christmas!

Kathy Carmichael

OTHER BOOKS BY KATHY

Below is a list of series and stand-alone titles by Kathy Carmichael. The Sweet and Cozy titles are "clean reads."

Texas Two-Step Series (Sweet Contemporary Romantic Comedy)

Western Pleasure Prequel — Book 1 — Novella

Chasing Charlie — Book 2

The Lassoed Bride — Book 3

Country Courtship — Book 4

Courting Trouble — Book 5

My Southern Bride — Book 6

Abby's Cowboy — Book 7

Christmas at Nelson Ranch — Book 8

The Cowboy Prince — Coming Soon

Line Dancing Bundle

Includes the first four Texas Two-Step stories: Western Pleasure, Chasing Charlie, The Lassoed Bride and Country Courtship.

Comedy & Cozy Bundle

Includes the first two Texas Two-Step stories: Western Pleasure and Chasing Charlie, and the first two Skullduggery Inn Cozy Reads: My Favorite Corpse and Mayhem on the Winterland Express

The Skullduggery Inn Series (Cozy Mystery)

My Favorite Corpse - Novella — Book 1

Mayhem On the Winterland Express - Short Story — Book 2

Suspects & Suitors - Novella — Book 3

Something Borrowed, Something Deadly - Novella — Book 4

Trouble Book Club (Sweet Contemporary Romance)

Here Comes Trouble — Book 1

Stand-Alone Titles

Contemporary Romance (Sexy)

Hot Flash

Cozy Mystery

Diary of a Confessions Queen - Amazon

Diary of a Confessions Queen - Other Retailers

Historical Regency Romance

My Lady Mischief (Sweet)

Paranormal Romance

It Happened One Christmas (Sweet)

Christian Nonfiction

Heaven and the Afterlife: Angelic Visitations, Near-Death Experiences, and the Loving Presence of Jesus. What Lies on the Other Side?

Holy Spirit: The Still Small Voice

It had been three days and Kelli Palmer couldn't seem to get the irksome cowboy out of her mind. Of course, his many phone calls might have had something to do with that.

She'd tried to remain busy by concentrating on her animal patients and by cleaning out her closet at home, but no matter what, she couldn't get the cowboy out of her mind. When she'd checked with her receptionist mid-morning, she learned Bobby Gray Nelson hadn't called today. She'd said, "Good riddance," but now she wondered.

Why hadn't he called?

Bobby Gray was giving up awfully easily. If Kelli had been intent on wooing a man—say, him—she wouldn't have given up after a few phone calls. She'd have considered it a challenge.

But then, that was the thing about her. She wasn't at all ladylike. She was determined. She was stubborn. And she enjoyed hard work more than she liked shopping.

Carefully carrying the small rabbit back into the examination room, she nodded at the little girl who owned the bunny. "Peter's fine. Only had a little indigestion and dehydration."

The child answered with a huge, gap-toothed smile as she clasped her bunny into her arms. "Thankth Docthor."

Kelli turned to the girl's mom. "You do know that Peter is short for Petunia, right?"

"Oh, no," answered the mother with a distressed expression on her face.

"Oh, yes. You'll want to bring her back for a pre-natal checkup in a week."

"She's pregnant?" asked the mother.

Using lay-person jargon, Kelli explained that the bunny would have her litter of babies within two weeks.

"Baby bunnies," cried the little girl happily, clapping her hands together.

Even the girl's mother wasn't all that unhappy. She smiled at the bunny and gave it a quick pet.

Kelli led them out to the waiting area and headed toward the next examination room, where someone was waiting with a—she checked the chart—sick kitten.

She clicked open the door, and stopped in her tracks. The cowboy in question stood there with one of the scrawniest and most active gray tabbies she'd ever seen.

Bobby Gray's face looked like someone had Sharpied eight thin, red stripes down it, but on closer observation, she suspected the kitten had meted out some feline discipline. Bobby Gray badly needed it, if you asked her.

"Mr. Nelson."

"So formal."

"Look, cowboy. I didn't return your calls for a reason. I'm not interested."

"You've wounded me again, Doc."

"You don't look the least bit wounded."

He held his free palm to his chest. "Can't you see I've got a dying kitten on my hands?"

The kitten's eyes were clear and alert. She glanced down at the chart, but didn't see anything there to indicate the animal was in jeopardy—other than being in the cowboy's possession, that is. He had probably brought the kitten in simply to get some time with her.

Some tiny part of her, perhaps her latent girlie-girl, was gratified that Bobby Gray hadn't given up. She liked persistence as a general trait, but it was a bad idea in his case because Lori wouldn't like what might develop between the two of them.

Kelli needed to send the man on his way, but couldn't resist first pointing out that she was onto his game. "The kitten may be a little skinny, but she looks healthy. I bet she's not even yours. Where'd you get her, the Humane Society?"

"I'm very attached to my kitten. Come here, Dolly." He pointed to his chin and the kitten licked it.

"So maybe Dolly knows you, but I'm not the only vet in the DFW area."

"The only vet I know," he lowered his voice, "and trust."

She wouldn't laugh. He was sooo bad. He was like dealing with a cute snake-oil salesman, if there was such a thing. Yet, at times she saw the man he could be lurking beneath the Stetson, and that was dangerous to her peace of mind. "What are your kitten's symptoms?"

"She's turned into an attack kitten. Watch a minute —you'll see."

He twitched his fingers in front of the tabby, and

the kitten raised her back and hissed. Bobby Gray grinned at Kelli expectantly while the kitten danced on the examination table. Too cute.

The kitten.

Not the loopy cowboy.

"You can take the girl out of Texas, but you can't take the Texas out of the girl." Born and raised in Dallas, **Kathy Carmichael** fondly shares that comment often. Her great-great grandfather, J.C. Lynch, was a cattle rancher and one of the first settlers in West Texas back when it was wild, and filled with Indian raids and cattle drives. Family stories about how her ancestor had met and married his beautiful Indian maid, and how the west was made, fired Kathy's imagination. There's little she loves more than the diverse Texas terrain and sitting outside on a sultry, moonlight night in Albany, Texas, watching the Fandangle with her family. The Fandangle is a musical, set outdoors on a lush rolling hillside. It's filled with old-time cowboy music, Texas Longhorns and other livestock, and locals reenacting the history of the settlement near Fort Griffith where J.C. Lynch had settled.

Kathy is a voracious reader and little appeals more than having her nose buried in a book. Her love for literature and writing, combined with her fondness for all things Texan, gives her a unique viewpoint. It was natural for her to blend these two loves when creating her Texas Two-Step series. Although the series is contemporary, the characters' backgrounds and outlooks reflect the principles of historic Texas and show how those principles remain part of their spirit today.

Kathy now lives in Florida with her Scottish husband, one son, one cat, three kittens and a herd of wild dust bunnies. She loves hearing from readers.

Keep in touch with Kathy
KathyCarmichael.com
kathy@kathycarmichael.com